T0113704

THE BOY WHO LOVED CAMPING

John Eppel

Pigeon
Press

Bulawayo, Zimbabwe

Published by Pigeon Press
12 Fortune's Gate Road, Bulawayo, Zimbabwe

For more information on this and other titles email:
info@hubbardstours.com

Cover Photograph: Violette Kee-Tui
Cover Model: Lucinda Patel
Cover Design: Anton Bhana
Text Design & Typesetting: Wayne Nel

ISBN 978-1-177906-144-7

In Memoriam

Margaret Hannan

Acknowledgements

I would like to thank Barbara Holmes, Cornelia Voigt, and Ben Eppel for helping me locate the London scenes.

I would like to thank Violette Kee-Tui, Paul Hubbard and Maureen van der Horn for their editorial assistance.

Finally I would like to express my grattitude to Ilan Elkaim and Paul Hubbard, both friends and former students of mine, for making this publication possible.

BOOK ONE
THE LATE FIFTIES

Chapter One

Dad was on the veranda playing darts with the cat. Mom was in the kitchen presiding over a beef stew, reading a cowboy book, and knitting a tea cosy. Ouma was in her room, halfway through her third Lion lager, whistling tunes from the War Years. Robyn was somewhere in the back yard spooning with her boy friend, Frikkie. Mercy had knocked off and was having an over-the-fence-conversation with the "girl" next door. Uniting these activities in a *concordia discors* was the voice of Richard Tauber, like a warm blade passing through butter, singing the Bach-Gounod *Ave Maria*.

Tom called out, "I'm home", and leant his fishing rod against the house. He smelled of nutrient-rich mud with a hint of orange peel. His muscular fox terrier, Jimmy, was with him, as always a greenish glow on his black and white coat, testimony to hours of fun in the algae encrusted dam, which was situated between the village and the Great North Road.

Dad unhooked Socks from the woven grass carpet. Hanging on the veranda wall, and circular in shape, it resembled a giant dart board. Even its pattern was conducive: alternating light and dark rings. Darts are thrown from the shoulder, but with cats, an underarm action is preferable. Darts are thrown with one hand, cats with two. Dad's method was to hold Socks with his claws facing the target, one hand supporting his neck, the other his rump. Cats are swung rather than thrown. Socks seemed to love the game, and would purr constantly, even when Dad missed the bull's eye.

"Hullo, son, did you catch anything?"

"A few tiddlers. I brought them back for Mercy's isitshebo."

Mom had turned the record over, and Tauber was singing, appropriately, *Pedro the Fisherman*. Dad swung Socks and he landed to the left of centre, a comfortable position for someone of his mildly conservative habits. For example, he preferred the sand box to the garden, gem squash to pets' mince, milk to ox blood.

"Dad, it's full moon tomorrow; can I go camping?"

"I don't see why not, son, but you'd better clear it with the Old Queen." Dad called Mom "the Old Queen" and Mom called Dad, but not to his face, "the Old Goat". Ouma was just "Ouma". She was Dad's grandmother, Tom and Robyn's great grandmother. She had been born in 1873, near the town of Barberton, South Africa; the daughter of smouse, Jewish pedlars who had followed the Voortrekkers. Ouma played the piano, drunk or sober, in the style of Winifred Atwell. She was known throughout the South-Western districts for her exhilarating rendering of *Dill Pickles*. In the distant past, she had supplemented Oupa's meagre income (he had been, *inter alia*, an engraver of hotel cutlery) by accompanying silent movies in the flea pits of Johannesburg.

Tom took the five tiddlers, threaded via their gills by a stem of love grass, to Mercy, still at the neighbour's fence, making noisy conversation with her friend, Comfort. "Izinkalakatha!" she laughed, graciously receiving Tom's offer, nevertheless

Mom called, "Dinner's ready. Wash your hands, Tom! Robyn, does Frikkie want to join us? Are you coming, Ouma?"

"Do you think that's Tauber whistling, Dad?" Tom asked as *Pedro the Fisherman* drew to its climax.

"I doubt it. Too undignified for a monocled German."

"Austrian."

"Same thing. Sis Tommy, you stink! You'd better have a bath after dinner."

"Same language, but..."

"You've still got bits of earthworm on your fingers. Use the nail brush."

Robyn and Frikkie wandered inside, holding hands, eyes like

saucers. Ouma, still in her room, two beers to go, was out-whistling Pedro. Jimmy yelped as Socks cuffed him smartly on the chops. Socks had been an old campaigner when Jimmy joined the family as a puppy, and she never lost her dominance.

"Whose turn is it to feed the pets?"

"I'll do it," said the obliging Frikkie. Reluctantly he let go of Robyn's hand. "Where's their dishes, Aunty Jane?" Frikkie was a strapping 16 year old boarder at Milton High School in Bulawayo. He was in form four. Robyn was slender like her brother, 15 years old, and a boarder at Eveline High School in Bulawayo. She was in form three.

"Al Jolson. Now there's a whistler."

"He was a Jew, like Ouma."

"Ouma's not a Jew, Tommy, she's Dutch Reformed, by St Paul."

"Dad, why do you always say that?"

"Say what? Robyn, go help the Old Queen with the dinner things."

"'By St Paul.'"

"We did *Richard the Third* for matric."

"So?"

"Robyn, go fetch Ouma. Well, Richard kept saying it and it kind of stuck in my head."

I knew that you must care was coming to an end. Tears were streaming from Mom's eyes as she placed the dish of stew at the head of the table for Dad to serve, though he never did. Mom leant over his shoulder and dished up from that position, always serving Dad first. By the time she got to serving herself, Dad, with a satisfied burp, would have flung his cutlery onto an emptied plate and pushed back his chair. Richard Tauber always made Mom cry, especially this song. She knew by heart the letter "of touching human interest", which was quoted on the record sleeve:

4

Dear Mr Tauber,

I sincerely hope you will forgive the impertinence of this letter, but I wonder if you would grant a special request. Three years ago a song of yours brought the man I love and myself together. It always remained a very special song to us. The reason I wish you to sing this song is, that lately we have drifted away from each other. If he heard you sing it, well, who knows he may think of those very happy days when it was recognized as "Our Hymn", and so unite us once more.

I know I am asking a great deal of a very busy man, but I do not think you will mind. The song is "I knew that you must care".

Thanking you in anticipation,

Yours very sincerely.

Robyn helped Ouma, incapacitated by her beer-steeped memories, to her chair. Before saying grace, she took a long swig from the last of the beers, thumped the bottle on the table, and croaked: "Dankie Heere vir my kos en kleere, maar my veldskoens maak ek self. Amen."

The beef stew was being served with rice, pumpkin, and broad beans from the garden. Dad eschewed all vegetables but he loved rice, and it was upon a miniature Mont Blanc that Mom ladled his stew.

"Like a golden dream..." sang the great tenor while the family and their guest tucked into Mom's cooking.

"Where are you sleeping tonight, Tom?" asked his sister.

"On the roof, I think. There's no wind."

"As long as you don't clomp around up there, son. I need my sleep; I'm working overtime tomorrow."

"I won't, Dad. This food is delicious, Mom." Frikkie concurred.

Jeremy Smith was foreman at the factory workshop. His hours were long: from 7a.m. to 5:30p.m. with a 40 minute break for lunch. His wife of 17 years would make him up a basket of sandwiches, fruit, and tea. She wrapped the sandwiches in a white table napkin, the bottle of tea in layers of insulating newspaper. She would leave the basket beside his breakfast things on the kitchen table, and go back to bed. Dad would get his own coffee and cereal while the family slept and the house creaked. Not infrequently, Tom was woken by the sound of a spoon clattering on an empty plate.

Dad stood up from the table and announced that he was off to bed. All except Ouma (who had begun to snore) bade him good night, and held out their plates for second helpings. It was the last weekend of the Easter holidays so there was a general feeling of impending loss, a kind of heart-heaviness, evident in the occasional sighs of Mrs Jane Smith: housewife, mother, knitter, and inveterate reader of cowboy books. Handel's *Largo* contributed to the mood as Side Two of *Memories of Richard Tauber* came sweetly to a close.

"Mom, can I go camping tomorrow night? It's full moon."

"Just the one night, Tommy. Your sister goes back to boarding school on Monday."

"Don't remind me, Mom," said Robyn, grimacing and feeling under the table for Frikkie's hand.

"And don't forget, there's the farewell dance at Jessie Hotel on Sunday."

"I won't, Mom, thanks. I'll take Jimmy with me. For protection."

"Tommy, he's not going to protect you from baboons or leopards!"

"Jimmy isn't afraid of anything-"

"Except Socks!"

"True," Tom conceded, "except Socks."

Mom got up to clear away the dinner things. Robyn and Frikkie rose to help her. Up the passage that led to the bedrooms a loud fart rolled. Everybody giggled. It was Tom's turn to get Ouma to bed.

6

Gently he shook her awake. Gently he wiped the spittle from her chin with his handkerchief. "Bedtime, Ouma," he said.

"Good morning, Jeremy," replied the ancient lady, "What's for breakfast?"

Chapter 2

Tom fetched the ladder from the garage and leant it against the rainwater tank. It was almost dark outside. A smoky red glow on the horizon had transformed the visible world into silhouettes. Mercy was gone – to the compound where she lived. Robyn was at the gate with Frikkie. Mom was undressing Ouma, helping her with her nightgown, putting her false teeth into an antiseptic solution, checking under the bed for zombies. Jimmy, his stump of a tail wagging, followed Tom.

The corrugated iron roof would not have been very comfortable without a mattress so Mom allowed Tom to keep one up there, as long as he brought it down if rain threatened – not likely at this time of year. It was one of those thin, black and white striped mattresses, stuffed unevenly with coir. Jimmy whined a little when Tom left him on terra firma, and climbed the ladder with a sleeping bag and pillow tucked under one arm. From the top of the tank he could easily climb onto the lower section of the roof, the gently sloping part above the kitchen. He shuffled, fully clothed, into his sleeping bag, positioned his pillow, tested the four sleeping positions, decided to start off on his back so that he could get lost in the milky way, lost with his dream: the Indian storekeeper's daughter.

Her name was Neela. She was in her early 20s, Tom calculated, and was studying for a degree by correspondence while waiting for a husband – by arrangement – from Gujerat province in that vast sub-continent which hangs like a uvula above the throat of the Indian Ocean. The white and off-white community to which Tom's family belonged referred to Mr Patel's shop as the Kaffir store. It was situated behind a general trading store-cum-butchery, which was owned by a Greek Cypriot called Mr Popadopoulis. Tom's people called this the European store. Mr Patel's shop had no

8

butchery but it employed a tailor and a shoemaker, both trained by Mr Patel, both in constant demand by the entire village spectrum. Tom had been on an errand for his mother when he first set eyes on Neela. She was sitting on the floor in a beam of sunlight sorting through a tray of sesame seeds for grains of sand.

Tom loved this shop for its gloominess, for the clicking hum of the sewing machine, in particular for its olfactory tones: brown sugar, bolts of cloth, paraffin, soap, bicycle tyres, bulk grains, shoe leather, and Mrs Patel's patchouli. Tom was fascinated by Mrs Patel's brightly-coloured, flowing saris, her gold bangles, and the mysterious red spot in the middle of her forehead. By contrast her husband was drab. When Neela began to help her parents in the store a new fragrance was added to the pot-pourri, a fragrance which intoxicated Tom. His errand had been to take Jane Smith's prized court shoes to the shoemaker. She wanted the heels to be rubberised so that she wouldn't slip again on the smooth concrete dance floor at Jessie Hotel. The Patels were fond of the polite young *gora* who spent all his pocket money, mainly on individually wrapped wads of pink bubble gum, at their store which smelled of Harpic toilet cleaner.

"Hullo, Tommy," said Mr Patel who was busy measuring two metres of cloth-a bold floral print – for a customer.

"Hullo Mr Patel...Mrs Patel. My Mom would like rubber soles put on her shoes so she doesn't slip and twist her ankle like last time."

"A wise decision. Why don't you leave them with me, Tommy, and I'll pass them on to Shoemaker when he isn't quite so busy."

"Thank you." Tom handed over the shoes. "And Mr Patel..."

"Yes, Tommy?"

"Who's that lady sitting over there?"

"My daughter, Neela. Would you like me to introduce you to her?"

9

"All right."

"Just let me deal with this customer, Tommy, and then I'll be with you."

Mrs Patel seldom spoke – her English was limited – but she gave Tom a broad smile and nodded proudly in the direction of her daughter. Sensing the attention, Neela looked up from her tray of sesame seeds, straight into Tom's eyes. Her beauty shocked the 11 year-old to the core of his being. She gave him a crooked smile and returned to her sorting, picking out the sand grains with nimble fingers and dropping them into an empty jam tin. An incongruous image appeared in Tom's head, of his father grooming Jimmy and Socks for ticks. He used a similar tin, a quarter filled with paraffin, to dispose of the parasites.

Mr Patel came over to Tom and motioned him towards his daughter. "Neela, my dear, may I introduce you to Master Thomas Smith?"

She looked up again, this time with a straight smile, and held out her right hand: "It's a pleasure to meet you, Master Thomas; I'm Neela – Mistress Neela."

Tom took her hand. It felt cool. "You hair is long," he croaked.

"Yes. I can sit on it."

"Like a horse's tail."

"I hope that's a compliment!"

"It's beautiful. You could play a violin with it. And you smell like..."

"Chandan."

"It reminds me of something."

"I rinse my hair every morning with a chandan pomade."

Tom still had her hand in his. He bent his head over it and sniffed. "Yes," he sighed. Gently she took her hand away and resumed her sorting. "Bye, Mistress Neela..."

"Bye, Master Thomas."

Tom was about to exit the store when he remembered something. He dug a coin out of his pocket and went over to Mr Patel at the counter. "Tickey bubble gum, please, Mr Patel?"

"Certainly, Tommy!" Mr Patel dug into the wide-necked glass jar and fished out six pink bubble gums in waxed paper wrappers. "Here you are, my boy."

"Thank you. Bye, Mr Patel, bye, Mrs Patel!" He looked quickly at Neela but she was absorbed in her grooming; then he ran outside into the sunlight, and proceeded to stuff all six bubble gums into his mouth.

He heard Robyn returning to the house, heard her exchange words with Mom, heard the toilet flush...felt socks kneading his chest through the sleeping bag, and purring like a distant tractor. His eyelids grew heavy. The kitchen faced west so he did not see the fat orange moon beginning to rise through the Mopani trees, its light putting out the stars one by one.

It had been weeks before he realised what her scent reminded him of: his father – the way he sometimes smelled. Tom nudged Socks off his chest, turned on to his side, curled his legs, and fell into a deep sleep.

Chapter 3

It was either Charles the rooster's crowing or the clatter of Dad's spoon on his breakfast plate that nudged Tom from his dreams into that space between sleeping and waking, which activates the creative imagination. He was sitting on the lichen spattered slab of granite, the topmost balancing rock of his favourite kopje. It had a cave with Bushmen paintings and Kalanga grain bins. It had spherical dolley holes. Scattered about its environs were potsherds, beads, flint tools, stabbing-spear heads, bullet casings and flattened bully beef tins. Halfway down the kopje, in a fairly level area of disturbed vegetation, were the remains of a settlement: the floor of a circular dhaka hut with pole impressions, and part of a stone wall, its chevron pattern still discernable.

Then she was with him, a heavenly blend of roses and sandalwood. They had the world to themselves, waiting for the moment when the setting sun met the rising moon. Their size is equal; their radiance is equal. The light of consciousness merges with the light of instinct. We sip our tea on the threshold of time and eternity. We are neither male nor female; we are perfection. "Like salt dolls, Master Tom, in the words of Ramakrishna...like salt dolls walking into the ocean, we lose ourselves together with the world..."

"Tom! Your porridge is ready!" called Mom from the kitchen door, "and it's your turn for the top of the milk."

"Coming!" Reluctantly Tom shuffled out of his cosy sleeping bag, flinching at the surface damp of morning dew. There was an early winter chill in the air. He carried the bag and his pillow off the roof, on to the rain water tank, and down the ladder. Jimmy was waiting for him, not only his tail but his entire rear end wagging. He greeted Tom with indescribable sounds of doggy joy.

The others had already eaten. Tom was alone at the table. He gave himself a small helping of steaming isitshwala - his mother made it softer than Mercy – and smothered it in sugar and creamy milk. "Thanks, Mom."

She had brought him a cup of tea. "I haven't sugared it yet. Here's a teaspoon."

"Thanks, Mom."

"When do you plan to go camping?" Her hair was still in curlers. She wore a white apron with a pocket in the middle wide enough to carry cigarettes, matches, and a paperback. It was one of J. T. Edson's *Floating Outfit* stories. Dusty Fog was Mom's favourite character.

"Mom, you're going grey."

"Don't remind me."

"How come Dad isn't and he's older than you?"

"Only by a few months. He's lucky I guess."

"Well, I think it suits you – makes you look distinguished."

"You haven't answered my question." She began the process of extracting and lighting a cigarette. She smoked a cheap brand called "Star", which came in packets of eight.

"Soon's I've finished breakfast. I need salt and matches and tea leaves and sugar and...Mom, can I take that little pot that pours?"

"I suppose so; as long as you bring it back, Tom. You know how careless you are with property." She held the cigarette between her forefinger and her middle finger. When she took a puff, her eyes narrowed. Tom watched the glow intensify, the ash tip lengthen. Her exhalation came out like a sigh. "And don't make such a noise with your spoon."

"Sorry, Mom."

Ouma began to sing something rude in Afrikaans. Her bedroom door was ajar. "Hoe ry die boda, finger in die hol, finger in die hol, finger in die hol...hoe ry die boda, finger in die hol, finger in die hol, hurrah!" Mom and Dad could both speak Afrikaans but they refused to translate Ouma's scurrilous versions of song and prayer for the enlightenment of the children. "I think Ouma's ready for her bath. Now, Tom, take care, and please come back early tomorrow. It's Robyn's second last day, and we've got the dance...*and*...we're having Sunday roast!"

"Roast! Yummy! Mom, do you think Dad'll mind if I take his Second World War sheath knife?"

"Just bring it back!"

"And his water bottle?"

"Ditto."

Jimmy sensed an adventure and he was beside himself with excitement. He stuck to Tom like a shadow as Tom packed his canvas haversack with supplies for a day and a night in the bush. Around the same shorts he had fished in and slept in, he added a stout leather belt to which he attached his father's World War Two water bottle and sheath knife. He didn't bother with a compass because he knew his way to and from this destination: a large kopje about eight miles, due north, from the rugby field. It was Tom's favourite camping spot, and he had even given it a name: Nowhere.

Around his neck he hung the rekken, which Mercy's oldest son, Ndaba, had made for him out of a forked Mopane stick, a piece of leather from the tongue of a discarded shoe, and strips of rubber from one of Dad's old tyre tubes. Tom used this weapon with deadly accuracy. In his pockets he kept smooth riverbed pebbles about the size of marbles. These were his bullets. He killed only for the pot or for protection. His biggest kills, respectively, had been a hare (on the golf course) and a banded cobra (in the chicken run).

He went to say goodbye to Mom and to Robyn and to Ouma, then he hoisted his haversack, redistributed his belt, and whistled unnecessarily for Jimmy. The road to the rugby field was of narrow dirt with a middle mannetjie sprouting coarse grass and stud thorns. Tom wore his thick-soled school shoes when he walked in the bush. He had learnt his lesson the year before when a vicious spine from a sickle bush had penetrated his tackie and lodged itself so deeply in his heel that Frikkie had to pull it out with a pair of pliers.

The soil here was alkaline and so poorly drained that the mopane scrub, smelling faintly of turpentine, formed pure stands on either side of the road. At this time of the year their leaves were turning yellow and brown. In the ensuing months they would be shed irregularly until, by the end of winter, they would be almost bare – waiting for the rains to transform them into things of beauty.

Jimmy trotted ahead of Tom, stopping frequently to mark his territory with a seemingly inexhaustible supply of urine. Every now and then he'd dash into the bush after a squirrel or down the road after a yellow-billed hornbill. He ignored the ancient woman who approached them, a large clay pot on her doek-protected head. Her smoky eyes had the light in them of regular contact with ancestral spirits.

Tom greeted her first: "Salibonani, Mama."

"Yebo, picanin baas. Linjani?"

"Ngiaphila. Ngingabusalina?"

"Ngiaphila."

"Abantwana banjani?"

"Bayephila."

"Kulungili, Mama. Hambani kuhle."

"Yebo, picanin baas."

She smelt of ash and mealie cobs; dust promising rain. Tom's observant eyes took in her bare, spatulate feet, her skeletal body partially concealed by a cotton dress that would not survive another wash. But she carried herself like a young woman, like Neela.

When he met Neela for the second time, she was sorting buttons. Tom asked if he could help and she showed him how to separate them into sizes and colours. She was sitting on an unopened sack of brown sugar and he sat as close to her as she would permit. She let him touch her hair, just once, and her sari, just once, because it was made of the finest silk. She explained to him why the garment left her midriff exposed. "The navel of the Supreme Being."

"God?"

"There is no name for it. The navel of the Supreme Being is the source of life, of creativity. The ancient Greeks called it omphalos, the centre of the world."

"In Ndebele it's inkaba."

"Yes; and the Shona call it guvhu. You see, Master Tom, it's situated in the middle of the body, a kind of threshold between the lower physical part and the higher spiritual part..."

"I don't understand."

"One day you will."

"What's a threshold, Mistress Neela?"

"It's a place that keeps things apart and together at the same time. Midnight is a threshold because it is neither night nor morning, but morning and night."

"He loved the clicking sound of the buttons as his fingers sorted them. "Mistress Neela – what's chandan?"

"Chandan is a threshold where the masculine scent of sandalwood blends with the feminine scent of roses."

"That's how you smell."

"Yes?"

"It's divine."

"Yes, Master Tom, it is."

They had arrived at the rugby field. Suddenly Tom noticed harvester ants bustling about with bits of dead grass in their jaws. Tonight's full moon may be hidden by clouds. Jimmy seemed more interested than usual in the ramshackle sports pavilion. He went sniffing at the door to the change rooms which, Tom knew, were kept locked. Tom thought he heard a moaning sound coming from within and wondered if, perhaps, an animal had been trapped in there. Nothing he could do about it. He whistled for Jimmy and they continued on their way to Nowhere.

16

Chapter 4

By the time they had reached the kopje it was clear that there would be no full moon that night. Most of the eastern sky was covered in cloud. The sunset, however, would be spectacular. Tom set up camp in the protection of the overhanging rock with its blood-coloured painting of a serpentine creature swallowing or discharging people at one end and venting or vacuuming people at the other end. He stored his equipment in the two virtually intact clay grain bins at the cave-like base of the rock; then he went in search of artefacts. There was always something new to discover in this historical treasure trove.

Once, Tom had taken some shards and beads home to show his parents. It had started a quarrel. Mom called it desecration; Dad said what's wrong with a few junk souvenirs. Tom put it to Neela, and she came down firmly on Mom's side. "Your Nowhere is a special place, Master Tom, a sacred place. Leave everything where you find it."

"Mistress Neela, will you come camping with me one day?"

"One day, perhaps." She was preparing a tray of tea and delicious Indian cookies for her parents, and Tom was invited to join them behind the shop counter where Mrs Patel's patchouli reigned supreme.

After tea they went back to sorting buttons on the sugar sack. Tom couldn't take his eyes off Neela's golden brown midriff. "Don't stare, Master Tom!" she smiled.

"Sorry, Mistress Neela. I was just wondering..."

"About what? Don't mix the two-holed with the four-holed, and throw out the broken ones. About what?"

"You know...the threshold. Belly buttons."

She laughed merrily. "There are three stages: the outside, the threshold or crossing-point, and the inside. You and I are on the outside; the Supreme Being is on the inside. When we cross over, we take off our shoes or our hats – or we crawl."

"If we are on the outside and the Supreme Being is on the in-side, what's in the middle?"

"Poetry."

"We have to learn a poem for school. Mine's called Cargoes by John Masefield. I already know the first verse."

"Will you recite it for me?"

"Okay." Tom cleared his throat, looked up at the bicycle tyres hanging from the ceiling, and began:

"Quinquereme of Nineveh from distant Ophir
Rowing home to haven in sunny Palestine,
With a cargo of ivory,
And apes, and peacocks,
Sandalwood, cedarwood, and sweet white wine."

"That's lovely, Master Tom..."

"Now you."

"Now me, what?"

"Say a poem."

"All right." She looked at Tom with her dark, melting eyes until he looked away. "This is by William Blake:

He who binds to himself a joy
Doth the wingéd life destroy;
He who kisses the joy as it flies
Lives in Eternity's sunrise."

"You have such a sad voice!"

Like the scrub robin that sings to the sun when it rises and when it sets; not because it sounded sad to Tom; on the contrary. At least it didn't make him cry the way Mom cried when she listened to

Richard Tauber; or the way Ouma cried when she played *Die Stem* in syncopated time on the Jessie Hotel's loose-stringed piano; or the way Robyn cried when Frikkie walked on his hands for her on the last night of the holidays.

While Jimmy chased rock lizards and leguaans, Tom scratched around for artefacts. He found a snail shell bead, a hand axe, and a crescent-shaped flint cutting tool. He left them where he found them. Then he went down to the spruit where water seeped throughout the year and where, later on, he would sit in wait for his supper. Where the sand was damp he dug a hole. He searched the dry bed for water-tumbled pebbles, projectiles for his rekken. On the granite slope which led up to the cave there were several bowl-shaped dolley holes in which he stored his "bullets". No one seemed to know who had made these mysterious bowls, or why. Tom's teacher, Handlebars (named for his moustache), thought they might have been used for milling foodstuffs, but he did not rule out aliens; Dad reckoned they were created by ancient prospectors; Neela wondered if they weren't natural geological formations.

When the sun began to set, Tom, with loaded weapon, settled himself below an anthill near the spruit. Jimmy stayed with him, knowing by instinct that he must not move an inch before the kill. Some minutes later, a male francolin appeared at the top of the ant-hill and began to crow raucously. At such close range, the pebble from Tom's catapult smashed its wing and it rolled down the anthill almost into Tom's arms. Expertly he broke its neck. He plucked it and gutted it right there. He washed the carcass in the five inches of milky fluid that had seeped into his water hole. Then he took it to his campsite where he prepared a fire on the ashes of his last adventure.

From a nearby lavender croton, still in full leaf, he cut three straight sticks, two with one forked end. He used these to erect a spit on which to cook the francolin. The horizontal stick, which fitted into the forks, was sharpened at one end so that it could easily skewer the bird. There was plenty of dead wood lying around and he had soon collected a sizeable heap. He used dried grass and leaves as kindling. It was nearly dark. A fine drizzle began to fall, too fine to put out the fire, which Tom watched, refracted, in the drops that gathered on his eyelashes. Jimmy lay curled up next to him – one ear cocked for danger. Tom dropped some fresh croton leaves on the flames and the smell of wood smoke sweetened to a fragrance which tapped his solar plexus.

She was siphoning into gin and brandy bottles, paraffin from a 40-gallon drum. Tom was corking the bottles. They had been talking about their fathers. "Well my dad isn't gentle, but he can be kind. He lets me use his Second World War things."

She was strangely animated: "Such as?"

"His sheath knife, his water bottle, his Italian bayonet...You know, he was a prisoner of war. Captured at Tobruk..."

"Really?"

"Yes. And he spent the rest of the war in concentration camps. He lost three toes from frost bite. That's why he walks funny. Have you seen his hands, Mistress Neela? They're huge. He can bend six-inch nails."

"What for?" She handed him another bottle to cork. Mr Patel was talking to Shoemaker about fish glue. Mrs Patel was replenishing the bubble gum jar.

"To show how strong he is. He's got arms like a gorilla."

"This paraffin is making me nauseous."

"Only one bottle to go."

The flames had died down sufficiently for the cooking to start. Jimmy watched with interest as Tom skewered the bird, sprinkled it with salt, and hung it over the coals. Very soon it gave off a delicious aroma. Tom wondered when insimba would appear. The dog would herald it with a low growl, but he had been taught not to disturb it.

Once the meal was ready, Tom built up the fire, which gave enough light in the pitch darkness (the entire sky was covered in cloud) for him to detect any nocturnal visitors. While Tom tucked into a drumstick, Jimmy waited patiently for his portion to cool sufficiently. At the bottom of the slope two bright eyes suddenly appeared, and Jimmy's mutter confirmed the arrival of a guest. Tom tossed his bone, and the small-spotted genet pounced. A ravenous crunching commenced.

When the meal was over, Tom offered Jimmy water in the cup of his hand, poured from Dad's battered World War Two bottle. Then he drank his fill. The fine drizzle had stopped some time before but it might return, so Tom decided to sleep in the shelter of the overhanging rock. The ground there was level and softened by a thick layer of dust, but it was unpleasantly close to a dassie midden. Since the air was completely still, he decided to let the fire burn itself out. Using his haversack as a pillow, Tom crawled into his sleeping bag and curled up for the night. Jimmy, one ear always cocked, curled up beside him. Somewhere in the distance a jackal yelped, and Jimmy's hackles rose.

Chapter 5

When Grandpa Percival died, Mom took the news badly. Tom and Robyn had huddled together in the lounge listening to her wrenching sobs. Richard Tauber had never done this to her. There was no telephone so the news had been brought by a messenger from the factory office, on a scrap of newsprint. Dad had been away, attending a meeting with the Directors at head office in Bulawayo. Tom was thinking of that day as he built another fire for his tea. Sometime during the night the clouds had lifted and the weather turned bitterly cold, too cold for anything but fitful sleep. To make matters worse, there had been a kill nearby shortly after Tom had climbed into his sleeping bag. To judge by the screaming and thrashing about, the prey was a baboon, the predator a leopard or a python. Jimmy had been restless all night long. But it was the freezing temperature that recalled to Tom his mother's story about Dullstroom, a small railway siding, which was known as the coldest point in the Transvaal.

Mom had grown up on a dairy farm outside Lydenburg. Her father provided the town with fresh milk and cream. When she was 15, she saved two little girls from drowning in the river, which served as the town swimming pool. She had been standing on the diving board when she heard a teacher screaming for help. "Anna and Elsie had been taken by the current. Neither could swim, and Anna was an epileptic..."

"You mean she had fits?"

"Yes, and she was having one in the water."

"But she didn't drown?" Robyn's eyes were wide with expectation.

"No. I dived in and swam to them. They were drifting quite quickly in the current. I managed to drag Anna to the opposite bank as it was closer. I went back for Elsie who was completely hysterical..."

"Did *she* drown?"

"Shush man, Robyn – let Mom –"

"You shush, Tom...go on, Ma...please?"

"You kids! No, she didn't drown either; but she ended up being more difficult to get ashore than Anna. In the meantime the teacher had sent a girl on a bicycle to fetch the doctor. Both girls recovered quickly from their ordeal. Anyway – Tom, stop picking your nose! – anyway, Elsie's father was the conductor on the train which travelled between Lydenburg and Johannesburg. He used to go as far as Belfast on the up-going train, and then he would get on to the down-coming train. Oops, I've dropped a stitch!" She was knitting a long-sleeve jersey for Dad, royal blue to match his eyes. It had a chain pattern.

"Between Lydenburg and Belfast there's a bitterly cold place called Dullstroom where you could get the hottest and nicest coffee in the world..."

"Mom, why can't we have coffee sometimes?"

"Because you're too young."

"Ah gee, Ma!"

"Do you want me to go on with my story?"

"Sorry, Mom; please go on?"

"Anyway, Elsie's father lived at the very bottom end of town, and the station was at the very top end, so he had to do a lot of walking. Nearly every afternoon Grandpa made a point of driving up the main street so he could offer Elsie's father a lift. He pretended that he had business at the station. He didn't want to embarrass the man.

"The following year I went off to the Technical College in Pretoria, and that's when Elsie's father started bringing me coffee on the up and the down trip, when the train stopped at Dullstroom. I was very embarrassed but this good man told me that hot coffee was the only way he could show appreciation for what Grandpa and I had done for him. This went on year after year, until I finished college, and then Dad and I got married and left for Rhodesia.

"When Grandpa died, 16 years later – early this year, you remember? – I had that very long and difficult trip to South Africa, and the last lap was the train journey from Johannesburg. The following morning, at Dullstroom siding, there was a rap on the compartment door and in came Elsie's father, with a cup of coffee. He put it carefully on the table, sat down on the opposite bunk, looked at me, and said in Afrikaans: 'Now our old friend has gone', and the two of us just sat and wept. Sometimes it really hurts to dig back into the past, and I do so often wish that I had been kinder to some of the people I knew."

Tom used three level pieces of granite to hold the pot over the flames. While he waited for the water to boil, he and Jimmy went to see if they could find any traces of the previous night's kill. The sun was still below the horizon but its first yellow rays were moving imperceptibly down the upper regions of the kopje. Tom was shivering with cold. They searched all the way round the rocky outcrop but found nothing. Tom decided to check how high the water had risen in his sand hole, and there they saw it, 15 feet long, with a lump in its midriff the size of a young baboon. Inshlatu. Now it wasn't only the cold that made Tom shiver; and Jimmy was positively vibrating. It watched them with a vertical pupil, its forked tongue testing the air, its spear-shaped head raised in defence. Tom was not the sort of boy to panic, and he knew that a python in the long process of digesting its meal was relatively harmless. It wasn't so much fear that he felt, but awe in the presence of this magnificent creature; and he thought of the ancient painting on the wall of the overhanging rock.

On the way home Jimmy had a wonderful time chasing kiewietjies on the rugby field, and Tom shot a rock pigeon for Mercy's isithshebo. He would prepare it for her and keep it in the fridge until she returned to work on Monday. As he passed the pavilion he listened for sounds of an animal in distress but heard nothing. He wondered if Dullstroom ever got as cold as Nowhere. He thought again of that day: his mother sobbing her heart out, his father far away, his sister clinging to him in the lounge, Ouma demanding her tea. Later he had gone to the Patels' store to break the news to Neela; but she wasn't there. She had gone to Bulawayo to choose a wardrobe for her forthcoming marriage to a stranger thousands of miles away.

Even before he reached the gate, Tom could hear Richard Tauber's honeyed mezzo thrilling the tree frogs with a song of old Vienna; could smell the crackling of a pork roast. Ouma was on the veranda with a bottle of beer in her hand. When she saw Tom she called out, "Hullo, boytjie, hoe lyk dit da'doer in die bosveld?"

Chapter 6

The Smiths had a pet budgie named Blue Boy. He lived in a cage in the lounge which was equipped with a bell, a mirror, and a cuttlefish. Opposite Blue Boy's cage, above the mantelpiece, was a framed print of Constable's *Wivenhoe Park*, a serene landscape with a lake in the foreground, trees in the middle ground, and a cloudy sky in the distance. It was a picture suggestive, not only of peace – the swans, the fishing boat, the cows grazing – but of freedom, and it provided Dad with a party trick which never failed to entertain family and friends, though Mom thought it rather cruel.

When the occasion was ripe, Dad would open Blue Boy's cage, and he would fly straight into the picture. The sky, the clouds, the still air above the lake, the grassy spaces between the trees – a two-dimensional illusion which all but concussed the desperate little bird – never failed to produce squeals of delight from guests.

Dad was tough. He'd had to be. He grew up on the wrong side of the railway line, mainly in the seedier suburbs of Johannesburg. Thanks to the itinerant nature of his father, a dealer in scrap metal who specialised in melted coins, he'd had to attend 11 predominantly Afrikaans primary schools, where the children did not take kindly to English-speaking Jode even though Dad was only half Jewish, and fluent in Afrikaans. When he was 13 his parents moved (escaped?) to Lydenburg, where he went to the same school as Mom, and where they became sweethearts. He was an apprentice fitter and turner when the war broke out, and he signed up for active service. Six years later, minus three toes, he completed his apprenticeship, married Mom, and went to seek his fortune in Rhodesia.

Lunch was roast pork with apple sauce, boiled potatoes, carrots, and cabbage. For pudding there was home-made ice cream

(Mom's speciality) with chocolate sauce. When Ouma wasn't confusing Tom with Dad, she called him Tommy-stront or Tommy-tier, depending on her mood. Today it was the latter because she was excited about playing piano at the Jessie Hotel farewell dance that evening. Dad, after a couple of beers, was in an expansive mood, telling them about the time he and a friend, both Boy Scouts, had cycled all the way from Lydenburg to Durban. They were 14 years old.

"You talk about being cold, Tom...we left in June, mid-winter... we had blankets, by St Paul, but our home-made canvas tent was no protection against the freezing temperatures."

Frikkie stopped chewing on a piece of crackling to ask, "How far was it from Lydenburg to Durban, Uncle Jeremy?"

"I don't know, exactly. About 600 miles, I'd say."

"Jeez!"

"From the start we struck bad weather, and the wind was against us, but by midday the wind had subsided and it was quite warm." He began picking his teeth with a split matchstick, and his eyes became distant with recollection.

"What make of bike did you have, Dad, a Raleigh?"

"No, it was a Rudge Whitworth, and it cost 10 pounds sterling. Dawid and I each had 10 shillings spending money. In those days 10 shillings went quite a long way."

"I only get two pounds for a whole term!" Robyn complained.

"Well, you come out quite well on it, don't you dear?" Mom got up to fetch the ice cream. She shrieked when she saw Tom's pigeon in the fridge. "It's bleeding into the milk jug, dammit! Tom, can't you do anything right?"

Tom hastened to rectify the situation. "Sorry Mom, it's for Mercy."

"Well, wrap it in newspaper or something; and give this milk to the animals."

"Yes, Mom."

When Tom returned to the table, Dad continued his story. "You see, Tom, I was also one of those boys who loved camping. In the evening, I remember, it began to get cold and windy again, and by the time we reached Machadadorp we'd had enough, and decided to camp a little way from the town – that's too much sauce! We pushed up the long hill leading out to Belfast, and at the top we found a road camp where, after obtaining permission, we pitched our tent, and had our supper. It was here that our first real bad luck began. Someone stole one of our knapsacks containing all the tinned food, and we only had coffee and sugar in the other one."

"I wish we were allowed coffee."

"Anyhow, we drank black coffee and went to bed. The next morning we took the road to Carolina, pedalling against a very strong, bitterly cold wind. I remember how grateful we were to some people who stopped their car to ask us directions to Carolina, and who gave us some oranges. It was late afternoon by the time we reached the town. We were starving, by St Paul, so we found a café and had a late lunch. When we told the Greek proprietor where we were going, he advised us to return home as the weather report, over the wireless, had predicted snow!"

"I've never seen snow."

"Nor have I."

"Look in the freezer."

"This ice cream is delicious, Mom!"

With a loud spoon, Dad worked through his dessert, and gave a satisfied burp. Mom helped Ouma from the table and took her to her room for a nap. The ancient woman broke into a song about her heart belonging to "die Boland, waar die blou, blou berges bly..."

Dad proceeded with his story. It was as if he had learned by heart some school magazine article he might have written about the adventure. "We ignored the Greek's advice and went on to Breyten where we pitched camp. The next day the weather was terrible. We barely made two miles per hour, when we should have done 10. As the day progressed the weather improved, the sun came out and warmed the cockles of our hearts. We went through Ermelo, Amersfoort, and, late that night, arrived in Volksrust – frozen to the bone, by St Paul. We were also soaking wet and filthy dirty. I remember us sitting on a pavement, talking, trying to decide where to sleep. We couldn't use our tent because it was sopping wet. So were our blankets. I don't know what made me do it but I went into a hotel and asked the price of a room and breakfast. The kindly lady must have pitied us, shivering with cold, because she allowed us to stay free! That night we had a hot bath and slept like the dead.

"Next morning we left very early. That's when I noticed that my bicycle lamp had been stolen..."

"Who do you think stole it? And your knapsack?"

"No idea; they just disappeared. Place was filthy with thieves. Now, where was I? Oh yes...

"It took us about half an hour to reach Charlestown. We pushed over Majuba, and so on to Newcastle. I remember how amazed we were at all those coal mines dotted about. And at Ingogo we saw two poor-white settlements! Natal was a lot warmer, and at Lady-smith, for the first time, we didn't have frost in the morning. We were chuffed, I tell you. Make no mistake about it.

"Eventually we arrived in Durban. We had been on the road for a week. Tom, cover your mouth when you yawn!"

"Sorry, Dad."

"Am I boring you?"

"No. Please go on. What happened in Durban?"

"Our first problem was where to find a place to camp. We were riding down a busy street, and I remember, every few seconds, a lighthouse lamp would flash over the town. At one point, when we stopped at an intersection, a boy of about 15, in scout uniform, rode up to us. He noticed our scout hats and asked us where we were from. At first he wouldn't believe our story but after we had convinced him he agreed to ask his scoutmaster if we could camp at the pavilion. Robyn, go fetch me a beer from the fridge, there's a good girl. His scoutmaster said that this would not be allowed but he suggested the Old Fort and offered to accompany us there.

"Well, to cut a long story short, we got permission from the caretaker to camp in the grounds. That night, when our tent was pitched and we lay under our dried blankets, I doubt whether there was a happier pair of boys in the whole world...thanks. Where's the opener? We didn't get up until about ten o'clock the next morning, and it was great not to have to tie our remaining pack. Janee, maak geen fout daarvan nie!

"All that day we loafed at the beach popping washed up bluebottles and burying ourselves in the sand. We had our meals in a café, but on...thanks, my girl...on the second day, one of the tenants of the rooms in the Fort invited us to supper, and this continued every night during our stay there. We had a great time in Durban and were well rested for out return trip."

"How long did you stay there?"

"About a week. On the last night we got everything ready, said goodbye to all the people of the Old Fort who had been so kind to us, and on the following morning we left for home. Jesus, Jane, can't you keep her quiet?

"This beer is a bit flat. Any-old-how, we were well on our way when we discovered that we had left our other knapsack behind! It contained all the food and a few of our spanners. On the first night we reached Howick where we inquired about an open space to camp. We were told to take a certain road, at the end of which we would find a site. Very much relieved we threw down our bikes and went to find a suitable spot for the tent. After climbing through a fence we discovered that adjoining our plot was a graveyard, the gravestones looking very eerie. Believe me, we shouldered what was left of our kit and virtually flew away from the spot!

"All went well with us until we reached a certain long hill between Estcourt and Colenso where...where are you going, Frikkie?"

"Sorry, Uncle Jeremy, but I need the loo."

"Off you go, then...er...in the distance of 100 yards, we had four punctures. The ground was so rocky. The only tarred roads in those days were in the large towns. Apart from this we had no further trouble during the whole journey; no further trouble, by St Paul."

Dad waited for the toilet to flush and for Frikkie to return to the table. Mom was battling to get Ouma to sleep. She was whistling an accompaniment to Eddy Fisher's *O Mein Papa*. Both Tom and Robyn were heavy-lidded. "We were very pleased to arrive in the Transvaal again, where we felt at home once more, but where we also had to face the terrible cold. On that last stretch we covered 100 miles in one day. Usually we did between 60 and 70 miles per day.

"When I think about it, we were more pleased to get home than we were to get to Durban. After all, we would get our regular food, and sleep in a bed!"

"Dad," said Tom, "why were you and Dawid afraid of that cemetery? The dead can't hurt you."

"I know, but in those days we believed in ghosts and all that, by St Paul."

"I believe in ghosts," said Robyn.

"So do I," said Frikkie.

"Well, ghosts or no ghosts, we'd better get some rest before the dance. Jane, are you coming?" As Dad got up to go to the toilet before his Sunday afternoon session with the Old Queen, Frikkie surreptitiously eyed the half finished bottle of beer that the Old Goat had abandoned.

Chapter 7

The Patels were vegetarian. Tom discovered this when he took them, wrapped in blood-seeped brown paper, two pounds of Mom's boerewors made from minced beef, minced game (kudu), and minced sheep's tail; flavoured with coriander, packed in intestines. Tom couldn't imagine food without meat. His most vivid memory of his grandparents' farm near Lydenburg was "killing day". They usually spent Christmas holidays at Spitzkop, but one year, for some reason, they visited in winter. One frosty evening, Grandpa, Uncle Boet, and Piriaan, the farm foreman, slaughtered an ox and two pigs. Tom and Robyn were allowed to witness the butchering. "After all," reasoned Uncle Boet, "you're going to help eat the buggers!"

The ox was wrestled to the ground by six labourers. It bellowed helplessly until the last seconds before its death, when it suddenly relaxed. This was the moment its head was positioned over a zinc bath, and its neck exposed for Piriaan. Before cutting its throat with a large, very sharp knife, Piriaan muttered something prayerful in Sesuthu. Tom and Robyn were shocked by the quantity of blood that gushed from the dying beast. After that came the disembowelling and the skinning: a messy affair.

The pigs screamed like human beings when uncle Boet killed them with a long, thin knife which went through their throats into their hearts. They had to be thoroughly bled before they died: a slow process. After they had been disembowelled, their carcasses were lugged on to wheelbarrows, covered in sacks, and soaked in boiling water. Then their bristles were scraped off with spoons and pieces of tin. Finally the carcasses were left to hang overnight for the meat to settle.

The next day, while the adults worked, the children feasted.

There was a big pot of sadza going, plus a few open fires. Each child was given a long fork, and meat offcuts were dished out freely. The prizes were the pigs' tails. Tom watched fascinated as some of the pigs' intestines were scraped and cleaned. They would be used as casings for the boerewors. The pigs' legs were pickled, later to be smoked – metamorphosed into hams. The shoulders and back were salted and dried; they would metamorphose into bacon. The best parts of the rest of the pigs, chops excepted, would be minced, which, mixed with beef mince and spices, would be transformed into droewors. What remained was cut into small pieces and rendered down in huge cast iron pots. These became lard and kaaings. The inside fat was very white and became leaf lard, which was used on bread and for baking cakes. Grandma called it "dripping". The second rate fat was put by for ordinary cooking, and the discoloured third rate fat was used for making soap. The kaaings, which Tom and Robyn loved, were bits of fat with meat sticking to them. They were rendered down, the fat was drained off, and they were kept like peanuts, in big tins. Add a bit of salt and pepper, and they made a perfect relish for the sadza.

The ox was separated into roasts, steaks, ribbetjies, chops, soup meat, stewing meat, biltong, mince...you name it. All changed, changed utterly or, as Ovid would have put it: "Now are fields of corn where Troy once was".

HOW TO TURN A BULL CALF INTO A BEEF OLIVE
First, by means of a suitable tool, turn the bull calf into an ox. Fatten the ox. Slaughter it, gut it and skin it. Hang the carcass in a cool room for a few days. Locate a retail cut known as topside (actually on the inside of the back leg), and remove a sizable chunk. Refrigerate until firm.
Cut into very thin slices. Pat out if necessary.

Prepare the farce. Finely chop an onion, a clove of garlic, and a sprig of parsley. Sauté lightly in butter before adding to the other ingredients. Chop three chicken livers and two rashers of rindless bacon. Season with salt, pepper, and a squeeze of lemon juice. Add a dollop of cream.

Mix ingredients and spread them on the slices of meat.

Parcel the slices. Secure with toothpicks or matches that have been sharpened on both sides.

Brown the parcels in a heavy-based saucepan.

Add vegetables of your choice. Set some brandy alight and pour it over the parcels. Cover saucepan with a lid, reduce temperature, and simmer until tender.

Serve with mashed potatoes and a salad.

Call them blindevinke, paupiettes, rolladen, involtini...call them beef olives. After all, what's in a name?

The closest the Smith family got to kaaings in Rhodesia were the off cuts around the butcher's block in Mr Popadopolis's General Trading store. These bits and pieces would have been tossed to the resident cat if Jane Smith had not claimed them for her frequent pot roasts. The bemused butcher was happy to give them away but Jane insisted on paying for them by the pound. "A pound of flesh please, Mishek?" and Mishek knew what she wanted.

When Tom offered Mr Patel the bloody parcel he said, "Thank you, Tom, but we don't keep pets."

Tom blushed and tried to explain that Mom's boerewors was made from the finest quality ingredients, and how difficult it was these days to get hold of a sheep's tail. When Mr Patel realised his faux pas it was his turn to blush, and then he explained to Tom that he and his family were vegetarians.

"Why, Mr Patel?"

"It's a long story, Tom, thousands of years long. You see, my family and I are Jains…"

"My Mom's a Jane."

"She is?" Mr Patel was astonished. "But why…"

"Actually, it's Elizabeth Jane, but she's always been called by her second…"

"Oh I see." Mr Patel was visibly relieved.

"No, Tom, our religion is called Jainism. We believe in ahimsa or non-violence, not just against our fellow human beings but against all living things."

"Even flies?"

"Even flies. Even mosquitoes, Tom."

"But, Mr Patel…"

"Even plants, Tom. Our religion forbids us to destroy those parts of the plant that are essential to sustain the life of the plant…"

"Close your mouth, Tom," said his mother's voice from somewhere inside his head.

"…like the roots or the stem."

"What do you eat, then?"

"Fruits, grains, vegetables, dairy products. We believe that, once the calf has been fed, the cow is happy to give us her milk."

Later, when Tom found an excuse to be close to Neela – she was stacking shelves – he asked her to elaborate. "Just the shirts, Master Tom, the trousers go on top. Thank you. It's bad karma to eat anything that has to be killed."

"What's 'kama'?"

"Not 'kama', 'ka-R-ma'. You are too young to know about 'kama'."

"So it's about sex?"

Neela's beautiful complexion went rosy with blushes. She busied herself stacking shirts, and made her reply to a size 17 collar: "Karma means 'action'. It's a Sanskrit word. You see, Hindus believe in reincarnation, Master Tom. That means the rebirth of a soul in a new body. If you practise bad karma, you get reborn in an unfortunate condition. It's a bit like that game, Snakes and Ladders...do you know it?

"Yes. We play it at home."

"Well, bad karma lands you on the snake's tail and down you go. Good karma lands you on the ladder, and up you go."

"Up where, Mistress Neela?"

"Eventually to a state of what we call 'omniscience'. That means 'all-knowing'."

"Like God?"

"Beyond God. Gods are frivolous. Bad karma. They bind us to the material world. Omniscience is liberation from the endless cycle of birth and rebirth. As I said, Master Tom, our souls have lived before in the bodies of other creatures."

"Like mosquitoes?"

"Yes. That's why our monks strain their water before drinking; why they wear gauze masks over their mouths; why they sweep the ground before them as they walk. It's bad karma to kill the tiniest creature even if it's done unintentionally."

"This shirt is missing a button."

"Well, leave it to one side, and Tailor will fix it. Do you understand me, Tommy?"

"I think so. I kill animals. I eat meat. I hate flies and mosquitoes...I've got a lot of bad karma."

"That's what we believe, though, personally, I'm not so sure. It's why so many of our people are traders. We are not permitted to do jobs which involve the taking of life."

"Like a soldier?"

"Yes. Or a butcher."

"Or a hunter."

When Tom got home that evening, he gave the bloody parcel to Mercy who clapped her hands with joy.

Chapter 8

The Jessie Hotel was where Mom and Dad first stayed when they crossed the Limpopo into Rhodesia. It was also known as Half-way Hotel: half way between Beit Bridge and Bulawayo. This hotel was the social centre for the scattered settler community in the south-western district of a country appropriately shaped like a teapot, the symbol of British colonialism in Africa: "Polly put the kettle on, we'll all have tea."

Highly polished semi-circular cement steps led up to a highly polished cement veranda, extending the full width of the white-washed colonial facade. Between the veranda and that part of the Great North Road (strip-tar) which connected West Nicholson to Gwanda, was a highly polished cement dance floor. It was round like a woman's waist, and it was girdled with shrubs and flowers. Two large trees in the vicinity, an African wattle and a wild fig, supported a criss-cross of electric lights in alternating colours of blue, red, green, and yellow.

The piano, which Ouma would soon be pounding, was located on the veranda, close to the pub. It was an old upright Chappell, badly in need of tuning. Waiters from Nyasaland, immaculate in white cotton suits, red fezzes, and car-tyre sandals, hovered about the tables as guests began to arrive for the farewell dance. The Smiths were on their way in Dad's two-tone Zephyr Zodiac. Ouma sat in the front with Dad; the back was jammed: Robyn on Frikkie's lap, Tom in the middle, and Mom next to the other window blowing cigarette smoke into the wilderness. Her talcum powder smelt of carnations, and it clashed with Ouma's 4711 cologne, Dad's English Leather, Frikkie's sweat, and Robyn's slightly sickly "Secrets of the Desert". Tom smelt faintly of the place where he had contracted slowly debilitating bilharzia, where he had once caught a barbel so large that it had fed Mercy and her family for an entire week.

Mom had refused to cook the mandevu. "You won't eat it," she had said; and she told him the story of the time she and Dad were fishing from the pont at Komati Poort. The pont was like a huge raft that ferried cars across the river. One Sunday, while they were peacefully watching their floats bobbing, the pont began to strain against its tethering ropes. Then it began to rock. "My picnic basket slid into the water, along with the latest Zane Grey – I think it was *Shadow on the Trail* – and Dad's pipe and tobacco pouch – he smoked Boxer Tobacco in those days – do you remember, dear? One of the natives, you see, had attached a chain to it, with a big hook at the end, and had caught a gigantic eel. It was about nine feet long and as thick as Dad's thigh. Well, Dad brought home a piece for me to cook. I went to a good deal of trouble over this eel. I cut it into thinnish slices, soaked it in bicarb water to be sure that it was clean, and then I fried it exactly as I did fish. It smelt good and it looked good, but Dad couldn't face it. He said all he could see was that great thick black thing writhing in the water. But I was sorry to lose my Western."

"Zane Grey!" snorted Dad. "What a load of rubbish!"

"You're entitled to your opinion, Jeremy, but..."

"Who was it who said the substance of a Zane Grey novel could be written on the back of a postage stamp?"

"Well I..."

"Now, Stuart Cloete is my kind of writer...or Robert Ruark. Frikkie, how did you get on with *Something of Value*?"

"I..."

"You what?"

"It was too thick for me, Uncle Jeremy."

"You like thin books, hey?"

"Not so thin, jis'...not so thick."

"Well, what about the book of Italian war heroes? Or the book of German humour? Those are pretty thin, by St Paul!"

Frikkie giggled appreciatively at Dad's jokes.

They passed the Geelong mine on their left and then turned into the grounds of the Jessie Hotel. Ouma began to whistle a medley of tunes all of which, and many more, would be part of the night's repertoire. Mom put out her cigarette in the car-door ashtray. Only Tom heard her sigh. Robyn set up a howl when she discovered that her gauze petticoat had been snared by Frikkie's belt buckle. Dad brought the car to a halt next to Wally Wallop's Vauxhall Velox, and they all climbed out, Ouma waiting to be helped by someone. It was a beautiful still night, packed with stars above and costume jewellery below. The nocturnal sounds were dominated by one-stamp mills, crickets, and giant eagle owls with pink eye-shadow. Soon they would be lost in Ouma's rendition of *Five Finger Boogie*.

Tom went to join his school pals who were wrestling each other on the slippery dance floor underneath the coloured lights. Robyn and Frikkie sought out the boarding school crowd who tended to lurk, especially pairs, in the less illuminated parts of the hotel. Dad made a beeline for the bar, and Mom helped Ouma up the steps to the veranda. The hotel owner, Mr Greenspan, welcomed them with a big smile, and ushered Ouma to the piano. In return for her playing, the hotel would supply beer on demand. Mr Greenspan had reserved a table for the Smiths near the piano. Like all the other tables, it came with a white starched linen cloth, an ashtray, a bowl of salted peanuts, and a waiter from Nyasaland. Mom ordered a Sedgwick's Old Brown sherry for herself, and a Lion lager for Ouma. The children would look after themselves. She had given them pocket money for cool drinks and snacks.

Since everybody knew each other, there was no standing on

ceremony, just lots of smiles and greetings, lots of "How are you, otherwise?" and "How's things?" and "Can't really complain", and "Isn't it a lovely night?" and "Did you hear the news?" and "You could of knocked me down with a feather!" Ouma's beer arrived in a tall glass. She whooped with joy. Someone from the bar shouted, "Tickle those ivories, Ouma!" and the ancient lady began. It was electrifying. Couples immediately moved to occupy the al fresco dance floor – Tom and his friends skidded out of the way – and they danced..."Oh, how we danced on the night we were wed..." she always began with a brisk waltz, singing along in her cracked old voice, pausing frequently to gulp Lion lager.

Soon only Mom, and a widow and a spinster, both teachers at Tom's school, were sitting at their tables on the veranda, sipping their drinks, smoking their cigarettes, and watching the couples footing it featly to Charlie Chaplin's *Anniversary Song*. Dad was holding the General Manager's 18 year old daughter, Penelope, so close that they could have held *The Best of Jolson* between them without fear of it slipping.

Ouma was playing *Heartaches by the Number* when Tom asked the Old Queen for a dance. She downed her third sherry and extinguished her tenth cigarette. They put their arms around each other's waists, Tom still a foot shorter than his mother, and made their way to the dance floor. Robyn and Frikkie were there, draped over each other, but Dad was back in the pub having a loud argument with a rancher called Jaap Engelbrecht. Jaap could load, single-handedly, 40 gallon drums of petrol on to the back of his truck; Dad could bend six-inch nails; so it looked as if there might be some extra entertainment in store for the settlers.

There was. When the drunken brawl started, Jaap "loading" Dad, Dad "bending" Jaap, Tom sought refuge in the sky. He found a quiet place near the water tank at the back of the hotel and lay down on his back. A certain arrangement of stars recalled for him the old woman with a clay pot on her head. There were combed lines around the neck of the pot, which looked like a child's depiction of water, or snakes. He had seen the same pattern on shards at Nowhere. Neela had told him about Aquarius, the Water Bearer, the eleventh sign of the Zodiac...

"Dad's car's a Zodiac. It's got six cylinders."

"When's your birthday, Tommy?"

"28th January."

"Then you're an Aquarian like me."

"When's yours, Mistress Neela?"

"Second of February."

"We're close."

"Aquarians are not materialistic. We are spiritual people. The water in the wise old man's pot is for quenching the soul, not the body. Sky water. Our flower is the orchid, our colour, electric blue..."

"Like my Dad's eyes."

"...Our trees are fruit trees, our gem stone, aquamarine..."

Frikkie found Tom, woke him, and told him they were going home. Tom followed him to the car and crawled into the back seat next to Mom. He didn't dare look at Dad hunched over the wheel. "All in, Uncle Jeremy," said Frikkie as Robyn settled on his lap, and Ouma began to snore. Dad started the car, stalled it, cursed, and started it again. Mom offered to drive but she was ignored. The car moved jerkily out of the hotel grounds and somehow found its way to the road home.

When Tom woke up for the second time his head was on Mom's lap. They were back home, in the driveway. He looked up to see Dad standing in the headlights, blubbering, Jimmy in his arms, too relaxed to be alive. Ouma woke up and immediately began to sing:

"The night seemed to fade into blossoming dawn,
The sun shone anew but the dance lingered on."

Chapter 9

"Neela, this is for you."

"Thank you, Tom, what is it?"

"It's a woer-woer."

She took the circle of string with a large button in the middle from Tom, and examined it carefully. "Is it a necklace?"

"No," Tom laughed. "It's just a toy. Let me show you." Tom took it back, thrilling at the brief contact with her fingers, fixed it on his thumbs and whirled the button round and round until the string felt tight; then he pulled, relaxed, pulled, relaxed; the button spun, the string changed into elastic. Woer-woer, it went; woer-woer, woer-woer.

Neela was fascinated. "Let me try," she said. She had a tiny mole on the left corner of her top lip. (Only Allah is perfect.) She squealed with delight once she got it going. They were sitting on the veranda wall outside Mr Patel's store, taking a break from counting stock. Customers came and went, their few coins securely knotted in soiled handkerchiefs.

Neela hadn't been at the store when Tom first arrived, mid-morning. "She shouldn't be long, Tommy," Mr Patel had said. "She went looking for driftwood and seed pods. She's working on a dry arrangement, a reminder of Africa, to take with her to India."

"Will she ever come back, Mr Patel?"

"Who knows, Tommy? Who knows?" He sighed the way Mom sighed, and returned to the gloom of the store.

Tom waited and waited. He was about to return home when he saw her in the distance, walking gracefully down the road which led into the village, beautiful to behold in her gently billowing sari. As she got closer he noticed that her hair was down, and as she got closer still, she began to put it up. At first she did not seem pleased

43

to see Tom, but she quickly perceived that he was distressed in some way, so she greeted him with a warm smile. When he asked her if she'd managed to find any driftwood, she looked down and shook her head. Then she asked him if he would like to help her stock-take, and he eagerly agreed.

"I also brought my Dad's Second World War knife to show you." He unsheathed it and offered it to her. She ran a finger down the groove of the blade. "You know what that's for?"

"What?"

"For the blood to squirt out."

Neela grimaced. "How dreadful!"

"Feel how sharp it is. My Dad's got an oilstone. Do you know how to play kennetjie?"

"No."

"It's easy. I'll show you." He jumped off the wall and proceeded to dig a groove in the earth with the knife. "We need two sticks, a long one and a short one." Neela pointed vaguely at the only tree in the yard, a syringa. Tom went to work, hacking here, cutting there. "This is the bat," he said, holding up a thin metre-length stick; "and this is the ball – catch!" He lobbed it at Neela, who almost fell off the wall in her effort to reach it.

Tom retrieved the short stick and placed it over the groove, which he then straddled, with the long stick in his hands. "Now, watch! I flick the kennetjie into the air and then hit it as hard as I can. The fielders try to catch it or stop it, and throw it back to the groove; the batsman tries to hit it away. If he misses it and it's less than one stick length from the groove, he is out, and it's someone else's turn. Come and field, Neela."

She slipped off the wall, adjusted her sari, and took up a fielding position. "Don't hit it too hard, Tommy; I'm only a beginner!"

"I won't. I'll give you an easy catch." He positioned the end of the stick under the kennetjie, flicked it into the air, took a swipe...

and missed. Neela stifled a laugh. "That means I'm out," said Tom, embarrassed; "it's your turn." He replaced the kennetjie across the groove.

They exchanged positions. She took the long stick, eased it under the short stick, flicked, swung, hit, connected, and the kennetjie went flying above Tom's outstretched arms, and landed with a clatter on the tin roof of the store. Mr Patel hurried out, looked bemusedly at the odd couple, and reminded Neela of the stock-take. "What is that hanging round your neck?"

"It's a woo-woo, a whirligig. Tom gave it to me. I'll show you how it works."

But Mr Patel's attention was riveted on the boy. "Tommy," he said, "what is the matter?" Tom had sunk to the ground, on top of the kennetjie groove; his chest was heaving with suppressed sobs. He couldn't speak.

Earlier that day, the boarders had been seen off at the railway station. It would take the steam train eight hours, stopping at every junction, to reach Bulawayo, which was less than 100 miles from the village. "Snot en trane," Dad called the occasion, as Robyn and most of the other girls wept, while the boys looked brave. Robyn was more than usually upset. She was not ready to forgive Dad for running over Jimmy in the driveway. She was sorry for her sadfaced little brother with his red rimmed eyes and his unkempt hair. She knew how precious the dog had been to him.

Dad helped Frikkie load her trunk and Frikkie's in to the coach which stored the heavy luggage, then he hurried off saying he had a job to do at the sports pavilion, installing metal lockers. He rumbled off in one of the factory trucks. Mom had made a basketful of tuck for Robyn: biltong, biscuits, sugared peanuts, and her favourite cupcakes with green icing. There was also a bottle of homemade lemon juice for the journey. The guard blew his whistle, the signal for final hugs, handshakes, and kisses, before climbing aboard. More children would be joining them in Gwanda and Bala Bala. With a whistle and a hiss of steam, the train chugged out of the station. The boarders were waved out of sight.

"Are you coming, Tom?" his mother called.

"Just now, Mom. I'll walk home."

"Remember you've got school tomorrow."

"I know. Worse luck." She lit a cigarette on her way to the car. Tom watched a halo of smoke form about her. He watched her drive away; then he walked the few hundred yards to Mr Patel's store.

"I've got something for you too, Tommy," said Neela. He wouldn't tell them why he was so upset but he quickly pulled himself together and went into the store to continue counting stock. From the folds of her sari she produced a little clay pot with a lid, and held it out to him.

Tom's face lit up. Thank you, Neela; did you make it?"

"Yes. It's the quintessence, Tommy. It's made from earth, and air, and fire, and water. Open it."

He already knew what was inside – chandan. The smell of Neela. Tears welled in his eyes and spilled down his cheeks. With difficulty he said, "Thank you, Neela."

She touched his forehead with the tip of her right index finger and said, "You're welcome, Master Tom. Now, hadn't you better be getting on home?"

He never saw her again.

Back home, he went to greet Mercy who was busy ironing in the garage. She clicked her tongue, gave him a big hug, and said, "Phepa bhakiti, Tommy." He fetched her the rock pigeon from the fridge, gutted though not plucked, and she thanked him and gave him another hug. The house seemed empty without Jimmy and

Robyn. Dad was on the veranda, drinking a beer and reading the Chronicle. He pretended not to notice Tom. Ouma was in her room, in her cups, whistling tunes of yesteryear. Mom was in the kitchen preparing dinner, a wooden spoon in one hand, a cowboy book in the other. Richard Tauber was in the lounge, singing *Bless This House* with a strong Austrian accent.

Tom asked Mom if he couldn't go straight to bed. He wasn't hungry and he was very tired. She agreed but first he had to have a bath. She'd left Dad's water in and it was still warm enough. After his bath, he climbed into pyjamas, climbed into bed, and lay on his back with the little clay pot on his chest. He was about to take off the lid when Dad sidled in. Quickly Tom hid the pot under the blankets. He braced himself.

"Son," said Dad, "Mr Wallop's dog has just had puppies, and he's promised me the pick of the litter." He approached the bed tentatively, raised a huge hand, which hovered before resting on Tom's head. Tom suddenly smelled Neela, and wondered if the pot had begun to leak.

Chapter 10

It was Tom's turn to recite his poem. A butterfly fluttered in his tummy. He waited for Doleen Vermaak to return to her seat, nostrils still flaring with a mixture of triumph and sentiment after an operatic delivery of *Young Lochinvar* – all eight stanzas. Mr Musgrave, himself a native of Caledonia, was deeply impressed, and when, in the climactic final stanza, he heard his own name declaimed:

There was mounting 'mong Graemes of the Netherby clan;

Forsters, Fenwicks, and MUSGRAVES, they rode and they ran...

(Doleen's emphasis), he bit off a portion of his moustache. He described it as a faultless performance and, there and then, gave the girl full marks: 10 out of 10!

As he made his way to the front of the classroom, Tom muttered "Prema, shanti, ahinsa". This was a mantra Neela had taught him to say whenever he felt nervous or afraid. She wouldn't tell him what it meant because that would remove its magic. He turned to face the class.

"All right, young man, get on with it!"

"Yes, Sir." Tom cleared his throat, looked up at a rainwater stain in the ceiling, and began:

"He who binds to himself a joy,

Doth the wingéd life destroy;

He who kisses the joy as it flies,

Lives in eternity's sunrise."

He started walking back to his desk. "Is that all?" Handlebars enquired, twirling the intact side of his moustache.

"Yes, Sir."

"But I've got you down for "Cargoes"! Come you here to me, m'lad!" Tom approached the Headmaster's desk, head bowed.

"Look at me, boy!" He looked at and then beyond the mutilated moustache to a poster depicting an exhausted Phidippides imploring the Spartans to help the Athenians at the battle of Marathon. "Explain yourself, Master Smith!" Twirl, twirl.

"I decided to change my poem, Sir."

"You decided? You?"

"It has a meaning, Sir; the other one…"

"The other one was just a little too long, was it not?"

"No Sir."

"Well then… face the class, and recite it."

"I…"

"Go on!" He gave Doleen Vermaak a conspiratorial smile.

Looking down at the splintery wooden floor, he began. His voice was muted: "Quinquereme of Ninevah…"

"Speak up. We can't hear you." The class giggled. Tom laboured through the first stanza and then gave up. Handlebars awarded him nought out of 10 and made him stand in the corner for the rest of the lesson.

"Right, Smith, you can turn around now. It was story time, time for Handlebars to read the next chapter of *The Black Arrow* by Robert Louis Stevenson. He gave his moustache a twirl, cleared his throat, and began:

"Er…Book Five. Crookback. Chapter One: 'The Shrill Trumpet'. Pay attention class! 'Very early the next morning, before the first peep of the day, Dick arose, changed his garments, armed himself once more like a gentleman, and set forth for Lawless's den in the forest. There, it will be remembered, he had left Lord Foxham's papers; and to get these and be back in time for the tryst with the young Duke of Gloucester could only be managed by an early start, and the most vigorous walking.

'The frost was more rigorous than ever; the air windless and dry, and stinging to the nostril. The moon had gone down, but the stars were still bright and numerous, and the reflection from the snow was clear and cheerful..."'

Tom's eyes wandered around the classroom walls with their familiar posters: Elizabeth Fry emerging from the Black Hole of Calcutta; Florence Nightingale ministering to the wounded British soldiers at the Crimea, her lamp held high; a youthful Cecil John Rhodes posing with a cricket bat; Phidippides imploring the Spartans; Julius Caesar crossing the Rubicon: Iacta alea est; Lord Clive of India...he wondered if Neela had heard of him, she seemed to know so much about the world. It was with a pang of jealousy that he thought of her husband-to-be somewhere in Lord Clive's country, coloured red on the classroom's world map, the same colour as Rhodesia and one quarter of the rest of the world. It would soon be break time...Mom's egg and mayonnaise sandwiches...playground games: kennetjie, slang, bok-bok-staan-styf, catches, French cricket, gaining grounds, running red-rover...Later that day, after school, the boys would go down to the dam for a klei lat battle, Baines against Selous...

...Selous, Selous, you can't spell 'boo'! Baines, Baines, you've got no brains!

The bell rang but Handlebars wouldn't let them go before he had completed the chapter: "'... the whole troop of chargers broke into the gallop and thundered, with their double load of fighting men, down the remainder of the hill and across the snow covered plain that still divided them from Shoreby.'" He shut the book with a flourish, and dismissed the class.

Neela had said she would have two wedding dresses, saris; a white one from her uncles, symbolising purity, and a red one from the groom's family, symbolising fertility. "And you know what, Tommy? – the bridegroom has to step on a clay pot and break it.

That's supposed to symbolise his potency."

"Potency?"

"Strength."

"I don't think I like that."

"I don't think so either...Then there are the seven steps."

"For each day of the week?"

"Or each deadly sin!"

"What do you mean, Neela?"

"Nothing, Master Tom; just joking. You see, fire is an important symbol in Hindu weddings. The bride and groom both walk seven times around the Sacred Fire. They take seven steps together. First step: to respect and honour each other. Second step: to share each other's joy and sorrow. Third step: to trust and be loyal to each other. Fourth step: to cultivate appreciation for knowledge, values, sacrifice and service. Fifth step: to reconfirm their vow of purity, love, family duties and spiritual growth. Sixth step: to follow principles of Dharma."

"What's dahma?"

"Righteousness."

"And seventh step?"

"To nurture an eternal bond of friendship and love." She looked, then, at Tom, and gave him the sweetest smile.

Chapter 11

The scandal broke during break-time. Tom and his classmates had gathered under the ancient lannea tree, which grew out of an even more ancient anthill. It formed a threshold between the school block and the playing field. They were eating their sandwiches and deciding what to do with their precious 20 minutes of freedom when Tracey White sidled over with her signature: "Have you heard the latest?"

The latest was that Andries van Blomensteen had been suspended for "doing it" with Mimi Jones. In his defence, Andries argued that it had been an accident. "We was playing catches there by the rugby field. I were on. I were trying to catch Mimi, but she tripped over a stone and I fell on top of her..."

"And then?" Twirl, twirl.

"Yissis, it just fell in."

"At the risk of being prurient [chew, chew], I must ask you, m'lad, how that could possibly have happened?"

"Her brookies was down."

"Did you pull them down?"

"No, Meneer, true's Bob – they fell down."

"Just like that?"

"The elastic sommer broke."

Andries was over-age; he had been held back because of an innate inability to achieve literacy and numeracy. He was the only boy who wore factory boots to school. In her testimony, Mimi had insisted that, "He made me do it, man!"

In a week or two, once the dust had settled, Andries, without permission, would clomp his way back to school, and then, "That fokkin Handlebars had better basop, jong!"

The boys decided to play running red rover. Tom, a fearless

tackler, was nominated and more-than-seconded to start in the middle. The others, eight of them, went behind an imaginary line at the far end of the field, which, at this time of the year, with the days closing in, looked more like a dust bowl than a turf. The rules of the game were simple: the person in the middle called out a name – a weakling to begin with – and the bearer of that name would attempt to run to the other end of the field. If the person in the middle managed to stop him, usually with a rugby tackle, he would stay in the middle and help stop the others. If he managed to get through to the other side, the others would shout "Running red rover", and storm across, conscious that one or more of them would be singled out for attempted tackling.

The girls had their own games: right now one girl was skipping while two others turned the rope, chanting:

"Down in the valley where nobody knows,

A bedbug stood on an elephant's toes.

'Ouch!' said the elephant, tears in his eyes -

'Can't you stand on anyone your own darn size?'

Others were playing hopscotch, ring-a-ring of roses, and the bells of St Clements. A few sat and watched the boys roughing it on the playing field.

Tom was about to call Wednesday Legs (when's dey gonna break?) when a large pair of steel-toed boots clomped into view. Andries was defying his suspension. "Call *me*, Smiff," he growled. Now Andries, being two years older than the other boys, and being naturally large, was a formidable opponent. Nevertheless, Tom called him. The bigger they are, the harder they fall, by St Paul! The boots came thundering down the middle of the field, right at Tom. One of the spectators screamed. Tom crouched low. If he tackled full on he would break a collar bone, or worse; so he waited for that instant when they were about to collide, ducked, and then dived. He took Andries behind the knees, slid down to the boot-leather ankles, and hugged with all his might. For a second he was airborne; then down they crashed, and ploughed to a halt. "Running red rover!" shouted the boys, and they ran for the other side.

They had a different version:

Down in the valley where nobody knows,

There stood Jane without any clothes;

Down swung Tarzan, bold as a brick –

Off with his cossy, out with his prick.

These words swam groggily into Tom's consciousness as he lay winded and apprehensive (Andries was beginning to growl) on the dusty playing field. Fortunately for him, Tracey White had reported the interloper's presence to the headmaster, who came storming out of the staffroom, cake crumbs on his moustache, with Miss Williams (of Wales), Miss O'Malley (of Ireland), and Miss Grundy (of England) in his wake. He ordered the "cretinous fornicator" off the school premises, and threatened him with expulsion if he returned before his suspension had expired. With muttered threats, at Tom, at Handlebars, at the world in general, Andries clomped away.

The game resumed. Tom limped to the middle of the field and called out, "Wednesday Legs!" The latter was easily despatched. Then *he* called out, "Georgy Porgy!" who was similarly despatched. Tom, with assistance, was just too good, and before break had ended, the entire gang was in the middle. They honoured Tom by singing about another hero, from a distant land:

"Born on a mountain top in Tennessee,

Killed a bear when he was only three,

Killed Handlebars with a carving knife,

Asked Doris Day to be his wife.

Davy, Davy Crockett –

King of the wild frontier."

A bell rang to signal the end of break, and Tom's class trooped into Miss Williams' room where they gathered round the piano to sing The Ash Grove.

Handlebars favoured the girls in Tom's class. There was no doubt about that. Was it because they were better behaved than the boys? Or was it because he liked to touch them? Mom told him of a teacher at her school in Lydenburg who also had a soft spot for the girls.

"He hated the boys but he was always ready to help us girls with our problems even when we did not have any. I remember he taught us Maths. We had single desks, and really there was no room for a second person, but he would squash up to us, put his arm around us, and fondle away. We were teenagers, so embarrassed, but too frightened to do anything, and we knew that every boy in the class had put down his pen, and was watching this teacher.

"He would call us up to the table, put his arm round our waists, and there was his hand, going up and down our bloomer legs -"

"Bloomer?"

"Bloomers were rather large pants with longish legs, and these had elastic in them so that they would stay up. There was one se- nior girl who complained, and guess what?"

"What?"

"She had to leave school."

"That's not fair, Mom!"

"No it isn't. But then life isn't fair." She sighed, put out her cigarette, and proceeded to light another. Once the tip was glowing she shook the match until it went out. Mom lived in a smoky world.

"He always sat at the table with his right elbow on it, and the left side of his body away from the table. We girls always had to go to the left side where he could put his arm around us and hold us close

55

to him. The boys had to go to the right side and, for sure, he wasted very little time on their books. My brother…"

"Uncle Boet?"

"Yes, Uncle Boet…once had the audacity to go to the left side. When this teacher's hand contacted khaki shorts instead of bloomers, he gave Boet a clout and sent him back to his desk."

"What happened to Uncle Boet?"

"He had to leave school."

"Jeez."

After the klei lat battle down at the dam, where Jimmy was more than usually missed, Tom went home via Mr Patel's store ostensibly to buy some bubble gum. Neela was nowhere to be seen. "Afternoon Mr Patel. Mrs Patel."

"Well, hello, Tommy," said Mr Patel, "how are you?"

"Fine, thanks, Mr Patel; may I have tickey bubble gum, please?"

"Certainly." The transaction was made. Mr Patel answered Tom's question before he asked it. "Neela has gone to Bulawayo. She is staying with relatives. There is much to prepare for her wedding."

"Will she come back?"

"Yes. For a short while, Tommy."

Chapter 12

"Hi Ouma, would you like to hear a joke?"

"Natuurlik, my skat. Fire away!"

"You see, there was this lady who owned a dog called Tits Wobble." Ouma chortled. "Well, the dog got lost, and she ran through the town crying, "Have you seen my Tits Wobble?"

Ouma cackled. "Tell that one about Shut up and Trouble."

"Again?"

"Again."

"Okay. You see, there were these two boys called Shut up and Trouble. One day they were playing hide-and-go-seek, and Shut up was on. A policeman came over and asked him, 'What's your name?' So he replied, 'Shut up.'" Ouma chortled. "Then the policeman said, 'Are you looking for trouble?' and he replied, 'Yes'". Ouma cackled.

"Say again that rhyme about Captain Cook."

"But Ouma, that's very rude."

"Nonsense. Say it!"

"Okay; but don't tell Mom."

"Say it!"

"Captain Hook did a poep
Behind an apple tree;
A piece of grass tickled his arse,
And then he did a wee."

"No, not that one, Jeremy, the Victoria Falls one."

"That's even ruder, Ouma!"

"Say it!"

"Um...Captain Hook went to the Victoria Falls...
He cut his cock on a piece of rock,
And a fish swam away with his balls."

Ouma nearly choked on her beer. Tom had to thump her on the back. "Come on, Ouma, it's not that funny," said Tom giggling. "Shall I tell you the one about a lady who had a dog called Deeper?"

"Say it."

"Well, there was this lady who had a dog called Deeper. One day she took him for a walk in the bush. A man jumped out and started raping her. She screamed for her dog to protect her calling 'Deeper! Deeper! Deeper!' The man cried, 'Yissus, lady, I'm as deep as I can go...'"

Ouma didn't find this joke funny. "Siestog, Jeremy," she said; "lelik."

Tom blushed.

Not as deeply as he had blushed the time he offended Neela. "What's a cocoon?" he had asked her.

"Well, it's a silky case."

"No, it's a k-kind of k-kaff…"

"Neela had looked at him sternly and said, "Master Tom, that is not worthy of you. What would your parents think?" Tom's cheeks burned and he dropped his eyes to the ground. Dad had told him the joke.

She had been working on an assignment for her degree, analysing a poem by Christina Rossetti. She was sitting at the shop counter surrounded by books and paper. "What do you think of this poem?" she said to a mop of brown hair.

"I'm sorry, Mistress Neela."

"Sorry about what? Look at me, Tommy."

He looked up, and there were tears starting in his eyes. "For saying that stupid joke."

"It's all right, Tommy, I know you didn't mean to be cruel; it's not in your nature. Listen: do you know what a mantra is?"

"He sniffed, wiped his eyes with his knuckles, and said, "No.""

"Well, it can mean a few things, but for me it's a very small poem, which you recite, over and over again when you are feeling anxious or sad. I keep my mantra a secret – even from a special friend like you."

"Why, Mistress Neela?"

"That's another secret." She gave him a smile, which turned his heart into butter. "Here, I'll write it down for you." She tore a page from her note book, and wrote: 'Prema, shanti, ahinsa'. Can you read that?"

"What does it mean?"

"Don't worry about that. Listen to it as you say it."

"I can't pronounce those words."

"Listen." She said them aloud.

"That's beautiful."

"Now you."

He said them, his eyes opening wider with each word. "Won't you tell me what it means?"

"No, because then it would lose its magic. But I can tell you what this poem means. Listen." She recited Rossetti's poem in a low, slightly tremulous voice.

Tom was enraptured. "It's a poem that makes you sad by telling you not to be sad."

"That is perceptive of you, but if you read it again and again, that perception will fall away."

"Why?"

"Because you are too conscious, too alert for intention. You need to let the poem carry you to the threshold, the no-place of dreaming."

"No-place?"

"Or Nowhere…"

"I see..."

"Do you know what cypresses are, Master Tom?"

"Trees?"

"Yes, and do you know what they symbolize?"

"No."

"Now *I'm* being too conscious, too alert for meaning...but sometimes...I don't know...sometimes it helps. How does Shakespeare put it? 'By indirections find directions out'. They symbolise death, Tommy. They are the trees of the ancient Greek underworld. They are planted in cemeteries all over Europe. And do you know what roses symbolise?"

"Love?"

"Yes. And love is the necessary opposite of death. Listen again:

When I am dead, my dearest,
Sing no sad songs for me;
Plant thou no roses at my head,
Nor shady cypress tree:
Be the green grass above me
With showers and dewdrops wet:
And if thou wilt, remember,
And if thou wilt, forget.

I shall not see the shadows,
I shall not feel the rain;
I shall not hear the nightingale
Sing on as if in pain:
And dreaming through the twilight
That doth not rise or set,
Haply I may remember,
And haply may forget.

See, Tom, it isn't about life or death, it's about life *and* death, about grass nourished from above and below – a condition of 'dreaming' evoked by the image of 'twilight' held in suspension. It's not science or history that threatens revealed religion, it's lyric poetry..."

Tom looked blank.

Chapter 13

Mr Musgrave was giving the class a lesson on the Zimbabwe Ruins near Fort Victoria. "Children, I believe I do not err when I claim that the Ruins were built by slaves...Van Bastárd, pay attention! – for the purpose of imprisoning slaves. Why do I not err?" Twirl, twirl. "Yes, Alice?"

"Because you have a degree from the University of Sterling, Mr Musgrave."

"Quite right, my dear. Quite right. Now, who can tell me who built the ruins? Alice, again?"

"Slaves, Mr Musgrave."

"That is not incorrect, Alice in Wonderland, not at all incorrect. Take it further, my dear: for what purpose?"

Many eager hands went up but Handlebars had his attention fixed on the strawberry blonde with baby blue eyes. "Mr Musgrave, for the purpose of imprisoning slaves, Mr Musgrave."

"Put it this way, pretty child..."stroke, stroke..."you are not wrong. Indeed, you are not wrong." His 'w' was faintly audible. He turned with a flourish to the blackboard, a piece of white chalk in his hand, like a sixth finger. "Write down this:"

THE ZIMBABWE RUINS WERE BUILT BY SLAVES TO
IMPRISON SLAVES

Tom wrote mechanically, his mind on other things. The end-of-term holiday was approaching; he planned to go camping further off in the bush than Nowhere, with his new pet, Rastus, a three-month old brindle bull terrier cross. If Neela was back from Bulawayo, he would ask her to go with him. She'd have to wear something more practical than a sari...Mom's overalls might do...

"HANDLEBARS!"

The chalk fell and broke into three pieces. The children looked up expectantly. "Ha, who calls?" from the Headmaster, swivelling. "HANDLEBARS!"

Outside, under the lannea tree, a pair of enormous steel-toed boots waited. Above the boots a pair of knotty knees with gravel burns from Tom's tackle. Above the knees, thighs like 10 gallon drums swaddled in token khaki. And so it went – all the way up to a chin that should have started shaving months ago. And the arms, brawny, held away from the body, fists clenched, at the ready.

An occupational hazard of school teachers is chalk dust. Not only does it clog your nostrils and your lungs but it slowly metamorphoses your body into a giant piece of calcium sulphate. If the Standard Five pupils in Mr Musgrave's class were not mistaken, their teacher, starting with his cheeks, was metamorphosing before their very eyes.

"Don't worry, Sir," said Thomas Smith, "I'll deal with this." Tom left his desk, and then the classroom, saying his mantra over and over. On the playing field a gang of pied crows were hopping in slow motion, like marionettes, looking for bread crusts. He stopped a few feet in front of the "cretinous fornicator", took a deep breath, and said, "What do you want, Andries?"

There were no close witnesses at this moment, so no one could say what happened first: fist on chin, or instep on balls. Both boys went down, one unconscious, one groaning "Jou fokkin moer!"

The groaner was eventually subdued by the United Kingdom (Scotland very much in the rear on this occasion, muttering, "Go off, I discard you,") while Tom, the side of his chin rapidly turning blue, slept.

"...why does the nightingale...I mean...why is it, like, in pain?"

"The nightingale is the voice of the poet, the poet with female sensibilities. Do you know the story of Philomela?"

"No."

"Well, her sister, Procne, was married to a brutal man called Tereus, King of Thrace. Tereus raped his wife's young sister, Philomela, and in order to keep her quiet, cut out her tongue. The gods took pity on her and turned her into a nightingale. To this day you can hear Philomela singing of her plight."

"Is that true, Mistress Neela?"

"All stories are true, Master Tom, even those that didn't happen, once upon a time."

"I love you, Mistress Neela..."

"I..."

Tom drifted back into the ache of consciousness. The first person he saw was Tracey White, and the first thing his ears picked up was, "Have you heard the latest?"

"What?" said England, who had been dabbing Tom's chin with a wet hanky.

"Fill us in," said Wales who was putting Tom's shoe back on.

"You're such a gossip, Tracey," said Ireland, who was offering Tom a drink of milky tea.

"Did I err?" inquired Scotland fiddling with his moustache.

Tracey paused for effect and then said, "You know that coolie who runs the kaffir store? Well, his daughter killed herself. She soaked herself in paraffin (in his mind's eye, Handlebars saw the double 'f'), and then she set herself alight.

"And do you know what else?" No one responded, so she continued: "She had a bun in the oven."

Tom sank back into unconsciousness.

Mom fetched him from school, one cigarette in her mouth and one, ready to be lit, in her hand. "I've got a bit of bad news, Tommy," she said. She had brought him another jersey to put on. The day was overcast and cold. The grey wool smelled of her fingers. "You know that funny little pot you keep on your bedside table?

Dad accidentally smashed it. I think he threw it at a rat or something. My God, Tommy, what was all that gunge? It's made a hell of a mess of your room, and I expect you to clean it up. Do you understand what I'm getting at?"

"Yes, Mom. Sorry."

"'Sorry' is not good enough, Thomas. When will you learn to act with responsibility? Why do you have to break your father's heart?"

BOOK TWO
THE MIDDLING SEVENTIES

Chapter 14

Hullo son,

I managed to get your address from Robyn and Frikkie – I thought you would want to know, first hand, that Ouma passed away peacefully in her sleep. She was over 100 years old – can you believe it? She will be cremated, and we have been given permission by Mr Greenspan to scatter her ashes in the garden of the Jessie Hotel – over the old dance floor, now cracked in many places and overgrown with weeds. Mr Greenspan says they'll soon be closing down and moving back to Johannesburg – you know, their son, David, was murdered by terrs a few weeks ago, and Mr Greenspan says they've had enough. So they too are joining the chicken run.

I've been very busy in the Police Reserve – setting up claymores around all the farm houses in the vicinity, and sandbagging the houses in the village. Things are hotting up – not that you would be interested. We arrested an ancient nanny whom we suspected of carrying food and intelligence to the terrs – in clay pots. The houts in my section gave her the thrashing of her life. The terrs have moved into Kopjes in the surrounding bush – twice the village has been subjected to rocket and small arms fire. So far, no one has been hurt, thank God. We got rid of Mercy because these people can no longer be trusted. Mom is coping very well with the extra housekeeping.

Which reminds me – Mom is thrilled to bits with the cosmetics you have been sending her – next thing I know, she'll be going down south for a face lift! At least it will give me a break from listening to Richard Tauber! As I write, he is singing A Little Love, A little Kiss, *and the Old Queen has moved the ironing board into the kitchen so that she can listen to her sweetheart.*

The kids went back to boarding school last Monday. These days the company provides a covered lorry to transport them – I was on convoy duty so I made sure they were in front. The road to Bulawayo has become very dangerous – no one stops at lay bys any more. We had the farewell party up at the club – dancing on the balcony – it was quite sad for me without you and Robyn. I got into a fight with Andries van Blomensteen – silly, at my age – I taught him a lesson

68

he'll never forget, by Saint Paul.

I've got a good joke for you – see, there was this Englishman, this Scotchman, and this kaff…

Tom quickly scanned the rest of the letter, crumpled it, and threw it away. Then he opened the one from his mother:

Dearest Tom,

I'm afraid your father finally got hold of your address, so you'll be hearing from him one of these days, I still don't understand why you won't communicate with him, after all these years, he is very hurt by this, it hurts me too that you never send me any letters, just parcels, not that I'm not grateful to you for all those lovely Elizabeth Arden products, my goodness, Tommy, how can you afford them, it's very kind of you, but if it wasn't for Robyn, we would know nothing about you. Poor Dad, he was badly beaten up by that nasty Andries boy, kicked him in the head and he had to have 12 stitches, also a black eye and some very sore ribs, he spent a night in Gwanda hospital, not too ill to flirt with the nurses, even the nannies. I'm busy reading Shane *by Jack somebody, so much better than the film although Alan Ladd is gorgeous, I must say. You won't recognise the house, security wire, and sand bags everywhere, Socks is not amused especially because now she's almost blind, she is over 20 years old would you believe and still eating her gem squash. The house is so empty what with Ouma gone, and Mercy, and you kids all over the world, isn't it wonderful news that Robyn and Frikkie are going to have a baby soon, I've started knitting, avoiding pink and blue, and looking at yellows and greens, which reminds me, did you take my nice tea cosy with you overseas? The fighting is getting worse and the whole world is against us, but I still say Rhodesia is Super!*

Ever your loving
Mom

He folded this letter and left it on the table. The last one, in a pink envelope, was from his sister, Robyn, all the way from Perth in Australia.

Dear Baby Brother!

We've decided that, if it's a boy, we're going to name it after its Uncle Tom! We haven't decided on a girls' name yet — Frik fancies 'Cheryl', but I'd prefer something more old fashioned, like 'Susan'.

I know that you're mad at me for giving Dad your address, but I felt so sorry for him. Do you know how Ouma died? She drowned in her own vomit after a drinking binge that went on for two days! I think Dad's mellowed a lot, Tom, and I wish you'd restore coms with him. Life's too short for bearing grudges. I still don't know what it is that turned you so violently against your own father. If it's Jimmy, that happened a long, long time ago, and he didn't mean to do it. I know he is difficult, and he gives Mom a bit of a hard time, but you musn't forget what he had to go through in the World War. Funny, though, he seems to be really enjoying our war. His letters are full of his exploits in the police reserve. He says he's invented a device for stopping vehicles at road blocks. It's like a three-dimensional metal swastika with sharpened points. You toss it onto the road and it always lands with one spike sticking into the sky.

Perth is full of 'when we's', like us. We tend to stick together because the locals mostly hate us, call us fascists and racists — it's very hurtful. They don't understand that our fight is against world communism not our black people. We've started going to church quite a lot. There's a Rhodesian minister not far from our neighbourhood who is very charismatic. He gets people speaking in tongues and throwing fits all over the place. He's actually quite famous, so you may have heard of him — Brother Moral Mac Braggert — ex Bulawayo. He reminds me a lot of Dad — same blue eyes, and nearly always dressed in a powder blue safari suit, with sweetly tapering espadrilles. No socks, mind you! He did a lot of sinning before he found Jesus — sex, drugs, communism...you name it. He says I've got cute dimples when I smile. You can imagine how jealous that makes Frik!

Anyway, that's all the news this end. Write soon.

Love

Robyn

Ps – I don't envy you cycling 20 miles a day to and from work in that weather!

Tom sighed, folded the letter, and placed it on top of his mother's. He would answer them when he felt a little less exhausted. There was half a can of Ambrosia rice pudding left over from yesterday's supper, and he forced this down his throat with a plastic spoon. He had run out of tea, and he had run out of coins for the metre. A single candle illuminated the dingy apartment in Crouch End. He was wearing two jerseys, an overcoat, corduroy trousers, three pairs of socks, long johns – and he still felt cold, not the bracing blue cold of Matabeleland, but the seeping grey cold of London, the kind of cold that got into your bones, and stayed there.

The apartment belonged to a secretive Libyan gentleman with IRA connections, who rented it to Tom for three quarters of his weekly wage. The previous tenant, an elderly widow, had died suddenly leaving most of her belongings behind. The apartment reeked: a bouquet of mildew, shoes, cat piss, and eau-de Cologne. These smells were concentrated in the bedroom, the sagging mattress in particular. Tom slept on the floor of the living room.

Eating out of a can, without an appetite, reminded him of his time as a rifleman in the Rhodesian army. Rat-packs. He smiled at the memory of those little tubes of processed cheese, which turned incendiary in the unrelenting heat of a lowveld summer. It was the only bomb he ever exploded. He recollected the incident which finally persuaded him to join the chicken run. For weeks they had been setting up ambushes at a suspected guerrilla entry point near Vila Salazar. Tom was fed up. Their platoon commander, none other than Handlebars Musgrave, decided to accompany Tom's section on their final patrol before returning to Bulawayo for de-briefing. How this middle-aged nincompoop had risen to the rank of second lieutenant was a source of bewilderment to the young men under his command. Tom thought it might have been because, with his new pencil-thin moustache, his short back and sides, and his tilted beret, he bore a striking resemblance to Monty of Alamein. He steadfastly refused to recognize Tom as his former pupil.

Handlebars decided they should spend that day looking for suspicious footprints. "Men," he said, "I believe I do not err [fiddle fiddle] when I tell you to look for a chevron pattern on the sole, and a check pattern on the heel. Think of the ruined walls of pre-colonial Rhodesia...think of Khami, of Dhlo Dhlo, of Naletale...think, men, of Zimbabwe. Those primitive patterns re-occur in the footprints of your terrorist [stroke stroke]. Do I render myself perfectly intelligible? I pause for a reply."

A few mutterings satisfied him and he scattered the five of them in all directions. For hours in the sweltering heat they searched the rock-hard ground for the tell-tale patterns. Eventually Tom saw a cow-hoof print in a dry gulley and called out, "Sir, I've got their trail!" Handlebars ordered the rest of the section to leopard-crawl towards Tom. "Look," he whispered, pointing to the cow-hoof print. The platoon commander blinked at it for a few seconds, and then he stood up, cocked his rifle, let off the safety catch, and took aim at Tom. He was deferentially restrained by the other soldiers, but back at headquarters, Tom would be in for the high jump. He spent a week in solitary confinement at Brady Barracks. When he wasn't running on the spot with his rifle held out in front of him, he was cleaning lavatory floors with a toothbrush. When he wasn't cutting down a buffalo thorn tree with a used razor blade, he was being beaten to a pulp by Rhodesia's heavy-weight boxing champion, lance corporal Andries "jou moer"van Blomensteen.

He blew out the candle and climbed fully clothed, teeth chattering, into his sleeping bag. His pillow was a rolled-up Milton High

School rugby jersey. Before curling into a foetal position, he groped around for Mom's tea cosy, and pulled it over his head. The cold would keep him awake for hours.

Chapter 15

The cold of early spring was nothing like the cold of winter which Tom had to endure when he first arrived in England. His single item of luggage, a backpack, was filled with camping equipment, and it was Tom's intention to get into the countryside before nightfall. He could not squander his precious 100 Rhodesian dollars on accommodation. He decided to head for Slough (which he thought was pronounced "Sluff") for the simple reason that his favourite drink was Horlicks, and he had known, from reading the label on the jar, that the Horlicks factory was situated in Slough. The warm, malted drink had been a Sunday evening treat at home for as far back as Tom could remember. But more special were the nights when he would wake up screaming, from a nightmare, and Mom would be there to comfort him. Lights went on, and the demons receded as Mom bustled about in the kitchen preparing him a soothing cup of Horlicks. The Patels also loved Horlicks. They had called it "the great family nourisher".

"'Haply I may remember,'" muttered Tom as he studied the map of London's Underground on a wall at Heathrow Station, "'and haply may forget'". He discovered, upon enquiry, that Slough was not far from Heathrow, but he needed to go into the city for two reasons. First, he had to register with an employment agency so that he could start earning some money; second, he needed food for the night, and he had heard that Trafalgar Square was infested with pigeons. He changed his Rhodesian dollars for pounds, 56 of them, and headed for Earl's Court Station. A friend of his in the army, who had worked in London, advised him to go to a place in Earl's Court called Industrial Personnel Services. They would find him piece work all over the city, and transport him there.

As it turned out, IPS refused to register him, since he was a fascist bastard; so he returned to the Underground and bought a ticket to Charing Cross; thence, a short walk through an underpass to Trafalgar Square. The place was teeming with feral pigeons. He seated himself next to one of the grim lions that protected Lord Nelson from French tourists, and surveyed the scene. He studied an old lady with bandaged legs feeding the pigeons bits of stale bread. They surrounded her, avoiding her unsteadily advancing shoes by the breadth of a hair. Tom had an idea.

He ambled over to the least populated part of the square outside South Africa House. He made sure no one, especially no official types, was watching him. Then he began to mimic the old lady. Soon he was surrounded by expectant pigeons. He shuffled forward for a while, marvelling at the way the plump birds rippled from his shoes as the soles came down. Then he took a sudden step back, bringing his heel down hard. A spume of pigeons ascended to safety, leaving behind one of their comrades with a broken wing. If anybody noticed, Tom would say it was an accident. Quickly he stooped, grabbed the bird, broke its neck, and, since there was no sign of bleeding, stuffed it into his coat pocket.

He wandered around for a while, looking at the statues, half expecting to see Richard the Third with "By St Paul" engraved on his plinth. He wandered off the square in the direction of the river, and came upon a pub out of which filtered a well known tune: *Danny Boy*. The style of the pianist was similar to Ouma's, and he felt a tug of nostalgia in the pit of his stomach. Impulsively Tom entered the pub, which was faintly lit by a few paper lanterns. It was almost empty at this time of day. Tom counted six men including the pianist, dressed alike in workmen's clothes. They were standing in a huddle round the piano, pints of Guinness in their hands; all turned to stare at the scruffy interloper, silhouetted, on the threshold. Tom wasn't sure if their stares were hostile or curious. He nodded a greeting to them, made his way to the bar counter, and ordered half a pint of Guinness. This was his first mistake. "Are you some sort of a feckin pansy?" The accent was thick Ulster.

Tom wasn't sure which of the men had spoken, so he replied to the lid of the piano: "It's all I can afford."

Tom's strange accent seemed to relax the tension. "Ah, Antipodean! Whereabouts?"

"Actually, I'm from Rhodesia."

After a long silence, during which Tom tensely sipped his creamy black beer, the pianist spoke, "Then you must be anti-Brit. Tell you what, mate, sing us a song, and we'll stand you the other half." His comrades seemed to think this was a good idea, and there were murmurs of approval.

Tom thought an Irish song would be appropriate, and this was his second mistake. He put down his glass, cleared his throat, and began, "'When Irish eyes are smiling, sure 'tis like a-'"

The piano sounded a harsh discord, the men growled; one of them, short and stocky with reddish hair and squinting green eyes, strode up to him, snarling, "Do you want to die?"

Tom was confused. "No, I...I heard you were Irish...*Danny Boy*... so I thought you'd like an Irish song..."

The man then unclenched his huge fist, and Tom noticed his ring – a gold skull and crossbones. He wagged this finger, with its cracked prints, an inch from Tom's nose, and said, "That's not Irish, that's feckin Anglo! Sing us an Irish song or you will not leave this pub alive!"

Now Richard Tauber wasn't the only golden tenor to have sweetened Tom's childhood. Richard Crooks came to mind, Beniamino Gigli, Jussi Bjoerling, Joseph Schmidt...even the South African, Webster Booth...but it was the great Irishman, Count John McCormack, upon whom Tom had modelled his own not unexceptional voice, who now came to his rescue. In his last year at boarding school in Bulawayo, Tom had won honours in the Eisteddfod competition for his rendering of Thomas Moore's sentimental song, *Believe Me if all those Endearing Young Charms*. He had listened to McCormack sing it countless times on the record player at home. He hoped it was genuine Irish. He whispered his mantra, took a deep breath, and began. The pianist was soon happily accompanying him, and it wasn't long before all the men were smiling.

"Believe me if all those
endearing young charms,
Which I gaze on so fondly today,
were to change by tomorrow
And fleet in my arms,
like fairy gifts fading away,
Thou would'st still be adored
as this moment thou art,
Let thy loveliness fade as it will,
and around the dear ruin
Each wish of my heart
would entwine itself
Verdantly still.

It is not while beauty
And youth are thine own
And thy cheeks
Unprofaned by a tear,
That the fervour and faith
Of a soul can be known
To which time will but
Make thee more dear.

No, the heart that has truly loved
Never forgets
But as truly loves
On to the close -
As the sunflower turns
On her god when he sets,
The same look which
She'd turned when he rose."

When the last note faded on his lips, there was not a dry eye in the house. Tom was going to live. By the time he stumbled out of the pub, he had an address to a hiring service in Fulham, which would turn a blind eye to his credentials; the name of a contact in Crouch End who would find him a place to rent; an old bicycle, a Raleigh Roadster, which he purchased for a mere five pounds from his new friend, the squint-eyed Paddy; and clear directions to Slough, a town which, he was assured, would not, for the time being, be targeted by IRA bombers.

Guided by red buses and black taxis, surely the most considerate drivers on earth, Tom wobbled his way to Fulham where he found the hiring service operating from a house in Crookham Road, Parson's Green. There a pleasant woman with red hair and green eyes made arrangements with him to report for work, the following Monday, at the Elizabeth Arden perfume factory in Wales Farm Road, North Acton. They required the services of a steam cleaner, whatever that may be. Tom asked the woman whose name was Maureen, if she knew anything about an apartment for rent in Crouch End; to which she replied, "Sure and *begorra*!" She telephoned someone called Amin, and chatted to him for a while; then she passed the handset to Tom; "Speak to the man himself," she smiled.

Tom learned from Amin that an apartment would be available

as soon as the old duck's body was checked out by the coroner, and then removed for cremation followed by interment at Highgate cemetery. She had died of hypothermia, nothing infectious. Tom made an appointment to meet Amin in the late afternoon of the following day. He understood that he would have to pay a week's rent in advance. Tom returned the handset to Maureen, thanked her profusely for her help, and took off for the town made famous by Horlicks.

Chapter 16

It was late afternoon by the time Tom had reached the outskirts of London, and it was already growing dark. He was tired and hung over, but pedalling at least kept him warm. Somewhere around Chiswick he located the Great West Road, which would lead him to Bath Road , the way to Slough. As soon as he passed Cranford he began looking for a place to camp, not easy in a region where signs like "Private Property", "No Entry", and "Trespassers Will Be Prosecuted", proliferated. Where Tom had grown up in Matabeleland, the bush began at your garden gate!

He envied the motorists who booked in at places along the road with inviting names like Travellers' Friend, Jolly Waggoner, and Ariel Hotel. He fantasized about hot meals and warm beds. He blessed Paddy for selling him a bike with a built-in generator. The headlamp threw a good beam on the tarmac in front of him. Past the Skyway Hotel, past Sipson Road T-junction, past Peggy Bedford, past Colnbrook...

The rapidly darkening sky soon made it impossible for Tom to pick out a place to camp where he might be safe from this nation of property rights. He began to feel desperate. Cars hooted at him to get off the road; the stench of exhaust fumes made him slightly nauseous; and he was so tired.

When he came to the M4 crossover, a freezing rain had begun to fall, and that decided him to camp in the underpass. He waited until there were no cars; then he got off his bike and dragged it up the sloping verge until he was no more than a metre under the pounding motorway. He shrugged off his backpack and sat, waiting for the traffic to thin, so that he could light his little gas stove and prepare his dinner. He retrieved the pigeon from his coat pocket, and proceeded to pluck it. "'And if thou wilt, remember,'" he muttered to himself, "'and if thou wilt, forget.'"

He went back to the night before his departure. Mevrou Marais, his old Afrikaans teacher, had invited him to dinner. She was a seasoned traveller, and she had some good tips for him. "Take long johns with you," she had said, "and never accept a drink that has already been poured from the bottle. You never know what they might have laced it with. More pumpkin, seun?" Tom politely declined a third helping of the sweet orange pulp flavoured with nutmeg. He wanted to keep some space for dessert, Mevrou's speciality: pumpkin fritters rolled in sugar and cinnamon. The Afrikaans teacher was no pushover when it came to pumpkin recipes. Her jaundiced complexion was a result, not of an obstructed bile duct, or of some liver disease like hepatitis, but of the regular consumption of enormous quantities of pumpkin.

"How is your drink? Let me banish the daylight from your glass." Tom gladly offered his glass for a refill. There was no denying the potency of Mevrou's home-made peach brandy, which she called mampoer, and which gave her nose a reddish glow. This, combined with her coppery cheeks, reminded many of her pupils past and present of the warm end of the visible spectrum.

"Another thing, Tommy – if you ever get the urge to spend a penny out in the open, do it through a sock. Otherwise your dingus will snap off." Although Tom had never seen real snow, there had been no shortage of literary snow in his colonial education, driven, flurried, and flaked by conscientious expatriate teachers. There were the 'snows of yesteryear'; there was the cherry, 'hung with snow'; there was Mary's little lamb 'whose fleece was white as snow'; and, in the bleak mid-winter of Christina Rossetti's bitter imagination, there was 'snow on snow, / snow on snow'.

"Which reminds me; I've got something for you." She bustled off down the passage while Tom sipped away at the liquid lightning in his glass. It was reciprocated by a real bolt from the sky, which, briefly, restored the daylight Mevrou had so hubristically banished.

81

She returned with a body belt made from one of her old bras. "Ja nee, that's where you keep your passport and your money." She showed him how to fit it around his tummy. She also gave him her copy of *London A-Z*, which was to prove invaluable.

Tom was gagging on his third pumpkin fritter when the lightning grew more intense, and the thunder: five, then four, then three, then two counts away. Down came the rain, up wafted the scent of Africa: sweetening dust. The temperature around the dining room table immediately cooled, and they both cheered the glorious downpour. Before departing, Tom helped the Afrikaans teacher put pots, pans, enamel basins, and other assorted containers underneath the many places where her house leaked; helped shut windows; helped comfort terrified pets; helped the old lady on with her much travelled raincoat, which she liked to call a mackintosh, since she had purchased it many years before in Scotland, birthplace of Andrew Murray, founder of her beloved Dutch Reformed Church.

With a "Lekker ry, seun!" Mevrou Marais, a childless widow then well into her 80s, kissed and hugged Tom goodbye. She accompanied him all the way to her gate. She was still waving when he turned the corner at the bottom of her road.

The traffic had thinned considerably. The rain, now Tom's ally, was bucketing down. It screened him from prying headlights, and it washed the plucked and gutted pigeon clean. Camping on a slope made everything a little more difficult, but Tom managed. He unfolded a wire braai fork, skewered the bird, sprinkled it with coarse salt, and held it over the naked flame of the little stove. The cooking smell was not as pleasant as that of the doves and wild pigeons back home. There was a hint of diesel, and something fishy. When it was ready, he turned off the stove and allowed a minute for the bird to cool. He ate it without relish – in both senses of the word, and then he prepared for sleep.

First he made a laager for himself with the bicycle and the backpack. Next he took off his army boots and changed his wet socks for two pairs of dry ones. Next he took off his coat so that he could put on a second and a third pullover. Next he pulled Mom's tea cosy over his ears. Finally he put his coat back on, buttoned it, and crawled into his sleeping bag. Within five minutes he was frozen to the bone.

There was nothing for it but to get up, put his boots back on, wait for the rain to stop, and cycle back to London. The rain did stop, after another freezing hour, and there was much less traffic on the road. Past Colnbrook, past Peggy Bedford, past Sipson Road T-junction, past the Skyway Hotel...Tom realised that he had to keep cycling all night; otherwise he might freeze to death. He decided to head for Crouch End.

Once back in the Greater London area there was sufficient electric lighting for him to consult Mevrou's A-Z. At Syon Lane, past Osterley, he turned right onto a smaller road, and then, soon, left into Kew Bridge Road. He recalled a poem he had learned in primary school, by Alfred Noyes:

Go down to Kew in lilac-time, in lilac-time, in lilac-time;
Go down to Kew in lilac-time (it isn't far from London!)
And you shall wander hand in hand with love in summer's wonderland;
Go down to Kew in lilac-time (it isn't far from London.)

At Kew Bridge he rejoined the main road, crossed the railway line, and veered left into Gunnersbury Avenue. He stopped to rest at Ealing Common, but only for a few minutes. The cold was unbearable. Beyond North Ealing the road changed its name to Hangar Lane. At the railway station he took the right fork into North Circular Road. This would take him all the way to Golders Green, which was not far from Crouch End.

At Stonebridge Park Station he checked his watch: 20 minutes after midnight. "Good morning, Mr Smith," he muttered to himself, "what price, free accommodation?" His backside was aching with saddle sores; his neck and shoulders were stiff from the weight of the backpack; he was on the point of exhaustion. At Neasden he got off his bike and pushed for a while, until the cold forced him back onto the saddle. He had to keep going. He said his mantra over and over again. Neela swam into his consciousness, her beautiful hair on fire, her navel blistering, her womb transformed into a baker's oven...but he forced her out, pushed her into the stars, the Milky Way...a southern sky.

He turned right a little too early, and found himself surrounded by countryside. A fox hesitated in the beam of his headlight, and then disappeared into a grove of silver birches. He was in Hampstead Heath. At Jack Straw's Castle he doubled back along Spaniard's Road. He didn't know then that this would be part of his route to the Elizabeth Arden factory in North Acton. The Spaniard's Road became Hampstead Lane. After Highgate he turned left into Hornsey Lane, which disappeared into Hornsey Rise. There he turned left and soon found himself in Crouch End. He wondered how long he would have to wait before he could get a hot cup of coffee. He recalled Mom's Dullstroom story.

He came to a final stop at a brick clock tower on Crouch End Broadway. He propped his bike against a stone placard at the base, which read:

ERECTION BY SUSBSCRIPTION
IN APPRECIATION AND RECOGNITION
OF THE PUBLIC SERVICES RENDERED BY
HENRY READER WILLIAMS ESQ SP
TO THE DISTRICT OF HORNSEY
DURING A PERIOD OF TWENTY FIVE YEARS
JUNE 1895

Shivering, teeth chattering, he walked up and down Crouch End Hill, waiting for the first café to open. It would be hours. That was Tom's first day and night in England.

Chapter 17

His first day at work was almost as dramatic as his first day in the country. He had to push his bike down every hill because his brakes wouldn't function in the rain. It was about ten miles from Crouch End to Wales Farm Road, and on that fateful morning a gale force wind had sprung up. Now Tom had purchased, from a bicycle shop in Crouch End, one of those plastic yellow capes, which cover, not only the cyclist but the entire bicycle. They keep out the rain and they resist the wind, resulting in exhausting slowing down or exhilarating speeding up.

Tom had been crawling along at about six miles per hour when the wind suddenly changed direction, and he found himself speeding along at about seventy miles per hour. To make matters worse, his cape flapped over his head to form a sort of mobile tent. For ten terrifying seconds, he was completely without visibility, completely without a sense of direction. Screaming his mantra, he braced himself for the inevitable – a head on collision with a car, or a wall, or a sturdy oak. Instead he landed in water. Apart from almost drowning as he struggled to extricate himself from the cape, Tom was unhurt. He discovered later that he had landed in the Leg of Mutton pond in Golders Green Pass.

He arrived at the Perfume Factory just in time to clock in. His supervisor, Aubrey Cheeks – Mr Cheeks to you – showed him to the change room where he was allocated a locker, a pair of white overalls, a pair of rubber Wellingtons, and an elasticised paper cap.

"We don't want no foreign dandruff in our products, now, do we?" Mr Cheeks gave him time to wring as much water as he could out of his clothes before reporting for steam-cleaning duty.

The ground floor of the factory was one huge assembly room broken into a number of units, circular conveyor belts, around which women, mainly of West Indian origin sat, putting lids on Elizabeth Arden products. The steam-cleaning unit was in a cubicle on this floor. Mr Cheeks showed Tom how to use the steam hose to clean the stainless steel containers out of which the various cosmetics were let into jars, bottles and tubes. It was a highly mechanised operation. The creams and the perfumes and the powders were easy to rinse but the lipsticks (in square plastic containers) required a solvent. Mr Cheeks showed Tom the solvent hose and urged him to use it sparingly. "Not cheap," he crowed, "by no means cheap." Washed items were balanced on a stainless steel table to dry.

Possibly to instil corporate loyalty into the young man from the colonies, possibly to continue enjoying the sound of his own voice, Mr Cheeks gave Tom a lecture on the great lady who had intoxicated the world with products such as Blue Grass, and Memoire Cherie. "Her real name was Florence Nightingale Graham. I don't suppose you colonial types have ever heard of our Florence. Founder of modern nursing, she was. Born in Canada, of Scottish parents. Colonial like you, come to think of it. Opened her first beauty salon on Fifth Avenue, New York. Changed her name to Elizabeth Arden. Watch out for them girls on the conveyer belts. Nothing but a bunch of fieves, the whole bang shoot of 'em. They called her The Lady and the Tramp. That's when she began to create her own cosmetics, didn't she? Moved into Europe, then Australia, South America...er...Crimea...The world was her oyster, I kid you not. Always wore pink. Owned racehorses. Went through husbands like toilet rolls, she did. Immaculate in white. Not just for whores no longer. Established makeup as necessary, absolutely necessary, for a ladylike image. The wounded soldiers worshipped her. Targeted old ducks and bags. Bunch of fieves, those darkies. Don't you trust 'em."

What Mr Cheeks lacked in coherence, he made up for with the

rhetoric of flesh. For example, his extraordinary rendition of the word "thieves" was accompanied by a facial judder, which squinted his eyes. During an ellipsis, his ears twitched. Every full stop came with outward flaps of both wrists. And when he went on to serenade "her grey eyes, pensive, yet ready to light into mirth", his knees buckled.

While Tom was helping him back onto his shoes he started reminiscing about the good old days when perfume was perfume, "not some bleedin' chemical, no, no, no!" Tom went on to learn how the factory used to import its fixative from East Africa, "from the bums of civet cats, I kid you not". The "natives" would trap these creatures in tiny wooden cages, and then torment them with sticks until they squirted "this muck, O it stunk to high heaven"; which they would scrape off the cage and tamp into cow horns. Once full, the cow horns would be plugged with coconut fibre and shipped off to "good ol' Blighty".

At last Mr Cheeks left Tom to get on with his work, which was already piling up. He started on a ten gallon moisturizing cream container. It was still about a quarter full of a divinely smelling substance Tom found out later was called Visible Difference, which sold in the shops for nine pounds a tiny jar! Now he washed more than two gallons of it into the sewers of London. He was battling with a lipstick tray when one of the assembly line women approached him. The pocket of her strawberry pink apron was bulging. She indicated to him to turn off the steam hose, then she went right up to him and whispered, "You're new here, luv; where you from?"

"Africa."

"You could've fooled me. Listen, dearie..."she dug both hands into her apron pocket and pulled out a bottle of Blue Grass perfume, two powder compacts, and four lipsticks in shades ranging from burgundy to pale pink..."these are for you. For your girl friend." She gave him a conspiratorial wink and pressed the items into his hands."

"Thank you."

"Shh!" She put a finger to her lips and winked again, pushing her cheek out with her tongue in a gesture that would have impressed the eponymous supervisor. "Don't mention it," she whispered; then she returned to her place, a unit which dispensed an artificial sun tan cream. Tom was touched by the woman's kindness. Only later, just before clocking out, did he learn that they were stolen items and had been given to him so that he couldn't report the factory floor "fieves", as Aubrey Cheeks put it. He too would be incriminated. From then on, at least once a week, a woman from the assembly lines would slip him a few cosmetics to sneak home. He made them up into little parcels and posted them to his Mom.

It was a lanky Nigerian called Sonny who warned Tom about the contraband. They were in the locker room changing out of their work clothes when Sonny noticed the items on the bench next to Tom. "Where did you get those?"

"One of the assembly women. She doesn't even know me. Isn't it kind of her?"

"Kind of her? Don't you see what she's doing? They all steal stuff, so they make you steal, so you won't rat on them." Tom looked at the cosmetics fearfully, and shuffled away from them. "It's too late now. But you have to hide them. There's a security check at the gate. If they find the stuff they'll fire you on the spot. It happened to my friend, Okonkwo. Those damn West Indians, they hate our guts."

Tom was battling to put on his still wet clothes. Sonny suggested he exit the factory in his overalls; then he could wrap the cosmetics in his clothes and in that way, smuggle them through the security check. His overalls were also wet from all the steam-cleaning, but not sodden; so he thanked Sonny for his advice, and returned to them. "Why?"

"Why what?"

"Why do they hate you?"

Because they blame us for selling them into slavery. How's that for bearing a grudge?"

Sonny was met at the gate by his beautiful blonde Swedish girl friend in a white Volvo station wagon. Tom, trundling his bike through the security check with his rolled up wet clothes on the back carrier, felt a twinge of envy. He determined to seek out a female companion as soon as he had a little money to spare.

Chapter 18

Weeks had turned into months since Tom's first arrival on English soil, since his winter of discontent. Now he marvelled at the transformation of spring: the sudden snowdrops, the overnight crocuses, the blackbirds singing from the tops of obsolete chimneys, the green tips on branches that had seemed as dead as sticks. The showers of April were nothing compared to the incessant rains of January. Cycling to work had become a pleasure. He even enjoyed the traffic. He learned to know when a Rolls Royce was approaching because all he heard was the tyres on the tarmac. He loved overtaking milk vans. He loved the friendly waves of bus drivers. These rooineks were not so bad after all.

He even started to love his job; and he was good at it. The assembly lines never had to wait for spotlessly clean containers. He made friends, the West Indian women in particular; they did not judge him for being a settler, but responded to his gentle nature. In any case, most of them had never heard of Rhodesia. They would come to work with empty tins of a cheap hand cream called Atrixo, and go home with those same tins full of Visible Difference, the factory's most expensive moisturiser. And every now and then one of them would slip a few articles into a pocket of his overalls.

He looked forward to the mid-morning break when he would march up to the canteen and exchange his coupon for a cheese roll and a cup of strong milky tea – the way Mom used to make it. He would squat on the floor with his fellow workers and chat about greyhounds and horses and football clubs. At lunch time he discovered something unique to English cuisine: three kinds of potato on one plate, leaving just enough space for overcooked peas and an item which looked like a sausage but tasted of layers' mash. Soon he began to spend his lunch break with Sonny, enjoying a pint of bitter at a nearby pub. Unlike the majority of women on the factory floor, Sonny was politically astute, and it was weeks before his initial hostility to Tom settled into a wary friendship. Tom attributed his belated political awakening to conversations with the Nigerian.

One morning, while Tom was hard at work cleaning lipstick trays, it occurred to him that the solvent he was using might get rid of the packed grease that had accumulated on his bicycle chain. He decided to steal some. The factory used little sample bottles to carry any product to the laboratory for testing, and they were kept on a shelf in the steam cleaning cubicle. Tom made the greedy mistake of filling two of these bottles with solvent, when one would have been enough to de-grease a dozen bicycles. He tightened the little black caps, and hid the bottles until knock off time. After that he worked doubly hard as a kind of penance for his theft.

Later that afternoon, when it was time to clock out, Tom sneaked the sample bottles into the locker room. There, while he changed out of his work clothes, he transferred them to his underpants, one on either side of his testicles. He walked carefully out to the bicycle ramps, and bent over to tuck his trousers into his socks. Now Tom didn't realise that these bottles were made of extremely thin glass. His bending action pressed the bottles together and both of them broke. The solvent seeped through his underpants into his trousers. It looked as if he had wet himself. Fortunately he had his yellow rain cape with him, on the mud guard carrier. Fortunately too, apart from a few pricks, he hadn't been injured – not yet. He straightened himself ever so slowly; ever so slowly, he got into his rain cape. Then, at a snail's pace, he pushed his bicycle towards the check out point.

It was a sunny afternoon with hardly a cloud in the sky. The security guard looked at Tom quizzically and said, "You expecting rain, guv'nor?"

"Not feeling well," replied Tom, "bit of a fever."

He certainly didn't look well. Every step he took something extremely sharp – left, right, front and back – threatened his genitals. "Get the missus to make you a hot toddy," said the guard, and he waved Tom through.

Tom sensed he was being watched as he laboured down Wales Farm Road looking desperately for an alleyway or any private space where he could assess and then rectify the damage. Eventually he found a spot partially sheltered by a stationary panel van. With his back to the world he shuffled off his cape, undid his belt, and gently lowered his trousers. What a mess! First he edged out the larger pieces of glass. He had to work with extreme caution. Next he extricated those slivers that had already entered his flesh and caused a little superficial bleeding. Fifteen minutes later, he was still pulling out fragments of the sample bottles. He wondered if the solvent itself might be doing some damage to his skin. He thought back to the times when, as a child, he'd come home from camping trips with Jimmy, infested with minute ticks, the size of pin heads. Dad would smother them in paraffin. Once they had died Tom would rub them off his body with a soapy cloth.

He was conscious of cars passing on the road behind him. He heard one slowing down. His heart began to thump. Then Sonny's voice, incredulous: "Jesus, Tom, are you having a wank in public?"

Tom pulled up his trousers and turned to face the white Volvo station wagon with the blonde Swedish beauty behind the wheel and Sonny in the passenger seat. Sonny was rolling down his window as Tom spoke: "Sure. It's more exciting. Especially when you're testing a new lubricant."

Chapter 19

Dearest Tom

Sad, sad news, you remember Mr Wallop who was transferred to Head Office in Bulawayo, remember he gave you the puppy after Jimmy died, well he is dead, murdered they think by terrorists, his body was found on the airport road, stabbed to death, poor Wally, he was such a kind man, they found his car abandoned at the airport, we couldn't get to the funeral but Reverend Jocks gave a beautiful service up at the club, we missed Oumas playing, we sang the 23rd Psalm and All things bright and beautiful and There is a green hill. There is also good news Tommy, your sister had a little boy and they've decided to call him Jeremy after Dad, Dad is so proud, he weighed 8 and a half pounds at birth, same as you, the war is getting worse, every day, raping, looting, rioting, every single day there is a combined operations communiqué announcing more deaths, honestly, all these communist terrorists on Rhodesian soil, do you understand what I'm getting at, my boy, it breaks my heart, and the world does not give a damn. Of an evening we sit out on the veranda and listen to the radio, Harvey Ward is such an excellent presenter, he says the Beatles are communists, I just wish they'd cut their hair!!! Afterwards we sing along with Mitch Miller. Anyway, time to get supper going, by the way, your last parcel arrived yesterday, that visible difference is doing wonders for my wrinkled old face, thank you tommy, be a good boy see, or should I say a young man!!!

Ever your loving
Mom.

Tom folded this letter and slipped it back into its white envelope. With little curiosity, he took his sister's letter out of its pink envelope, and read:

Dear Proud Uncle

The Lord has blessed Frik and I with a beautiful baby boy. We decided to name him Jeremy after his grandfather. I had a good labour, considering it's my first child. And my darling husband was there to witness the miracle. I wish you could see him now in his green cap and yellow booties, knitted by his doting grandmother.

Mom is also knitting for the boys in the bush, balaclavas mainly, and socks. Dad is still very active in the police reserve, says he's notched up his first direct kill but doesn't go into details. In all his letters he writes about how much he misses you even though you have treated him so badly. Thomas, he forgives you. Please restore coms? Tell him you are sorry. Tell him you love him as the Lord loves you. In the words of St Luke: "Joy shall be in heaven over one sinner that repenteth, more than over ninety and nine just persons, which need no repentence".

Frik and I are also doing our bit for Rhodesia, albeit from a safe distance. We have joined The Christian League of Southern Africa, which was started by Father Arthur Lewis, a truly saintly man. Dad sent me a cutting from the newspaper, which I'd like to quote to you. It's Father Lewis responding to the murder of 27 black tea workers by communistic terrorists. I hope it shakes you up a bit, Thomas!

This was an act of sickening, cold-blooded barbarity. It shows Marxists in action - the deadly enemy - not only of Christianity, but of humanity. This will be the fate of the black people in Rhodesia if order and civilised standards are not maintained. The defeat of this evil thing, Marxism, must be the aim of every man and woman of every race in the country.

We've broken away completely from the World Council of Churches, which is nothing but a front for communism. If you'd like to enrol as a member of the C.L.S.A. I've got some spare coupons. Just say the word Thomas –BE GUIDED BY THE LORD – and I'll send you one.

I'm glad you have settled down to your job in England and that you have

made some friends.   Oops, Jeremy's crying for his bottle, and Frik is at Bible
Study.   Must end.   God bless you, Thomas.   Write soon.
   Your sister in Christ
   Robyn, Frik, and Jeremy

Tom tore this letter into little pieces, climbed into his sleeping
bag, and fell into a profound sleep.

Chapter 20

One late afternoon, Tom decided to visit Highgate Cemetery. He passed it every day on his way to work. From the road, it looked more like a park than a graveyard. He was immediately attracted by a huge black bearded bust, which seemed to be staring at him. From an illustrated version of Mark Twain's *Huckleberry Finn*, he recalled the visage of that notorious con man, the "King". Tom lay down his bike and approached the tomb of – he was shocked to discover – Karl Marx. It was strewn with red flowers: plastic, silk, and real. Of the last named, some were buds, some were blooms, and some were blown. Here was Rhodesia's arch-enemy, adored; here was the communistic terrorist, idolized; here was the world's most evil man, worshipped. What's with these people?

He moved closer to the granite pedestal so that he could read the inscriptions: 'Workers of all lands unite': that seemed pretty reasonable; 'The philosophers have only interpreted the world in various ways; the point is to change it'. Mmmm – that seems a bit drastic. Certainly changed my world. The bronze bust, which had stared at him when he was on his bike freewheeling down the road to the entrance of the cemetery, was now a good six feet above him, staring still at all manner of travellers on the Highgate Road.

Seeing that polished stone and feeling its cold hardness on his fingertips reminded Tom of a time he went prospecting with his childhood friend, Jacob. He smiled to himself as he recalled their excursions into the bush, not primarily to hunt, but to look for 'precious' minerals. Jacob was Mercy's son. He wasn't allowed in the house but he was most welcome to play in the garden with piccanin baas Tom. Today the friends were going prospecting. Each carried a small sample bag. Around their necks dangled rekkens for taking pot shots at flying and crawling creatures. Their trousers pockets were bulging with 'bullets', suitably sized pebbles, which they had been collecting in the Smith's driveway. Tom was allowed to take his dad's sheath knife for combat and general utility, while Jacob proudly carried his father's knobkerrie. Mercy provided them each with a packed lunch consisting of peanut butter and syrup sandwiches, and generous slices of home-made apple crumble.

Dad had already left for work; Mom was lighting a new cigarette from her old stompie; Ouma was in the scullery listening to L.M. Radio featuring 'Be My Love' sung by Mario Lanza. A tree frog holding on to the door jamb out front began to pour forth his soul. A loosely attached water pipe somewhere in the plumbing system was knocking. The combined sound forced Mom to block her ears, and the boys to exit the yard with alacrity.

They headed for a river bed, dry most of the year, which fed into the village water supply. Scattered over the fine white sand were the shells of crabs and other crustaceans, and pieces of driftwood, much favoured by the likes of Mrs Ally Wallop, who transformed them into dry arrangements which would gather dust in her home and the homes of her friends. The boys always took one or two pieces back for her. But they were more interested in searching for specimens of AMAGUGU, their fantasy gems, more precious than diamonds. In reality it was any pretty stone they managed to find along the banks of the stream: calcite, jasper, rose quartz, agate – even pieces of shiny, river-tumbled serpentine.

Along the way the boys played a word game called inky-pinky. A nonsensical definition in English had to be rephrased in rhyming Fanakalo. 'You go first, Jacob.'

'Okay. Let me see…"More medicine".'

'That's easy: "Futi muti". Now me…"Get to work".'

'Something "Sebenza"…Got it: "Enza Sebenza".'

'Correct.'

'You won't get this one: "The woman knows the farm".'

Tom thought for a while but couldn't get it. 'I thought so,' chuckled Jacob. 'It's "Umfazi asi ipulazi".'

'Clever. How about, "Go and catch the snake"?'

'Putsy. "Hamba bamba lo mamba". What about "There's a fish under the water"?'

'What's "fish"?'

'"Inhlanzi".'

Tom thought for a while, then his face lit up and he said, '"Nanzi inhlanzi phansi lo manzi".'

'Right.'

' Here's a long one for you…er…"Don't cry when I kill the old man".'

Jacob couldn't get it. At that moment his sharp eye caught sight of a leguaan, about half a metre long, sunning itself outside a crevice in a granite ledge. 'Kangela,' he whispered to his friend. Silently they removed their rekkens from around their necks, felt in their pockets for a "bullet", loaded, took aim, and fired. One stone zinged off the rock but the other went home sending the reptile scurrying for shelter.

'"Haikona kala skat mina bulala lo madala".'

The first thing they did when they arrived at the river bed was to gobble their sandwiches. Something tickled Jacob's lip. He felt for the cause, pinched it between finger and thumb, and extracted a hair, which Tom identified as Ouma's. Their slices of apple crumble the boys scattered for the birds and the ants. Tom passed round his father's water bottle, filled with lemon cordial, and they took long swigs. After that they set about looking for AMAGUGU. Jacob took the left bank, Tom took the right. Whenever one found a particularly pretty piece, he showed it to his partner, who was always generous with compliments.

When their sample bags were full they looked for a place to rest before the long walk home. They lounged under the partial shade of a kudu-berry tree, its leaves, this late in the year, taking on fiery colours ranging from yellow to red. '"Agree to leave while talking about biting".'

'" Vuma puma kuluma luma".'

'"Lie down and wait while you write for free".'

'"Lala sala bhala mahala".'

Jacob rummaged about in one of his pockets and brought out an almost empty bag of Boxer tobacco. 'Buya tina bema,' he said.

'Ipi wena tolili lo ma gwaai?'

'Mini chonchili yena.'

'Sure?'

'Sure nyanisi.'

'Ipi?'

'Ubaba omdala.'

'Uncle Sifasa?'

'Yebo.'

'Bantu bakithi!'

They used the brown paper of Minny's sandwich packets to roll the tobacco into cigarettes. Jacob kept two or three matches and the striking surface of a match box behind his ears, which he now utilized in the lighting of their brown paper tubes stuffed with a mixture of dried pawpaw leaves, dried cow dung, and Boxer tobacco. The first puffs resulted in violent coughing but after a while things settled down, and the friends lay back and stared dreamily at the patches of sky beyond the ragged canopy of the kudu-berry tree.

The walk back to the Smith's place was punctuated by pot shots with their catties at almost anything that moved. The acacias here grew in thick clumps. Many of them were exuding gum which the

100

boys sampled as they trekked. It tasted like postage stamps. Beside an anthill where a greater variety of trees grew, and there was a particularly dense shade, they surprised some juvenile impala that bounded off in all directions. Using Jeremy's knife, they carved their names together in the trunk of a pod mahogany.

It was in a clearing that housed electricity pylons, creosoted blue gums, that Jacob brought down a crimson-breasted shrike. It had been feeding its young. He felt bad afterwards, and insisted on burying the creature where it fell. 'Mina kona sorry maningi,' he whimpered, 'sorry maningi.' Tom found a large chunk of granite nearby and lugged it over to mark the grave. He put an arm round his friend's shoulder and guided him out of the bush.

Marx's tomb, egregious in Tom's eyes, was surrounded by many lesser graves, some adorned with pretty angels in stone. He wandered about the place, lovingly cared for, teeming with flora and, he would notice as evening descended, fauna. A strange sense of peacefulness settled in him, strange because he was the only living soul in this garden of the dead. Shouldn't he be edgy? He found a wooden bench and sat down. Presently he began to feel entombed in the amber light of this northern sky. Something brushed the sleeve of his shirt; something whispered – a sound made hollow by the proximity of tombstones; something nudged his shoe. He looked down and saw a hedgehog negotiating the obstacle. There must have been a pond nearby because he heard frogs plopping. Then out from a clump of dandelions a rabbit emerged, then another. Tom looked up and saw the first stars, a rare sight in London, beginning to twinkle. An image of Neela sitting on a sack of brown sugar, sorting sesame seeds, appeared and disappeared. He thought of the old woman, the water carrier, who had passed him on the road to Nowhere. He thought of Jimmy trotting ahead, suddenly dashing into the bush after a squirrel or a butterfly, returning with a pretended limp, sniffing about the sports pavilion, his tail wagging as if there was someone he knew inside. He recited his mantra, and his tears were checked. He stood up and went to find his bike. On the way out he turned to give Karl a wink. 'No hard feelings,' he muttered.

Chapter 21

The next day Tom got fired from his job. He was lucky not to be arrested. Shortly before knock-off time, one of his West Indian friends slipped him two powder compacts. Instead of going to the locker room to secrete them, he went to the far end of the factory floor where some other toilets were located, ones used by more senior personnel. Mr Cheeks was at the urinal writing his name in water. "Well, if it isn't my young colonial friend. Don't you know this is where the big knobs hang out?"

"Sorry," replied Tom, "I was nearby, and needed to go." He was acutely aware of the hard flat cases, burgundy coloured, in his overalls pocket. He sidled into an unoccupied toilet and closed the door. He sat on the seat and waited for Mr Cheeks to depart. Mr Cheeks shuddered, shook, buttoned, and clomped away, whistling one of Ouma's tunes – *Lily of Laguna*. Tom's hands were shaking while he transferred the loot to his underpants. He pulled the chain, ran a tap at the basin, as if to wash his hands, picked up the tune, and walked out singing: "I know she likes me, I know she likes me, because she says so [click, click], she is my Lily of Laguna [click, click], she is my lily and my rose [click, click]."

As he walked past the first assembly line, all the women turned in his direction and one of them called out "Ooh, bionic an' all!" She gestured towards his crotch. The compacts in his underpants had metamorphosed into castanets. He stopped, blushed, smiled sheepishly. He still had the entire factory floor to cross. And there ahead daring Tom to continue , was his ever-suspicious supervisor, Aubrey Cheeks.

Now Tom tried to walk in a way that would keep the compacts from making contact, and this gave the impression that he was still desperately in need of the toilet. He had to pass his supervisor in order to return to the steam cleaning cubicle. With ribald laughter behind him and Mr Cheeks' leer in front of him he felt trapped between the monster Scylla and the whirlpool Charybdis. He got an idea. If his walk suggested that his bowels were about to burst, why not exploit the suggestion, and in that way effect an escape? He gave Mr Cheeks a desperate look, bent over, and clutched his stomach. Then he turned and made his way back to the toilet, transferring his hands to his backside as if desperately containing the imminent explosion. Behind him there were screams of laughter.

Safely inside the lavatory, Tom removed the compacts from his underpants and put one in each of his overalls pockets. Then he sat on the lid of the WC and waited. Ten minutes later he repeated the routine of pulling the chain and washing his hands. He emerged to an expectant factory floor. When he saw Mr Cheeks still there, waiting for him to pass by, he knew he was in trouble. The fact that he no longer clicked seemed even funnier to the women on the assembly lines than when he did click. This time the laughter was accompanied by applause. Tom played along and took a couple of deep bows.

"I think I do not err," said Aubrey Cheeks as Tom walked past him, "that you are confining on your person, certain contraband, goods forbidden to be supplied by fieves [squint] to...er belligerents..."

"Excuse me?"

"I put it to you, young colonial, bearing in mind that I am a veteran of the Last Effort wif six medals to prove it...I put it to you that you are in possession of stolen goods. Come this way, please." He took hold of the collar of Tom's overalls and marched him to the security guard at the gate. "Search this man!" he ordered.

The stolen compacts were soon discovered. Tom was escorted to the locker room where he changed out of his work clothes. He gave his remaining tea coupons to Sonny who solemnly shook his hand. The women on the factory floor were no longer laughing. The one who had slipped him the compacts looked distressed. Tom waved them good bye and a hundred hands waved back. His bicycle was confiscated but they allowed him to take his yellow rain cape. Mr Cheeks warned Tom that if he asked for severance pay he ran the risk of being arrested. Did he think they didn't know that he'd been working illegally [twitch]... "er"...[flap]?

It was a crestfallen Tom who set about walking the ten long miles back to Crouch End. The trees, now in full leaf - planes, horse chestnuts, silver birches - the early flowering hawthorns, the fruity scent of elderberry, the chirruping of small birds... none of these now held any attraction for our hero. He had no transport. He had no money (he had given his last few coins to a beggar). His six month visa was soon to expire. What was he to do?

Three hours later, the clock tower came into view. Wearily he ascended the steps to his apartment – rent was due soon – and lay down on top of his sleeping bag. He would spend the night there, and, early the following day, make his way to the West End. Perhaps his IRA friends would help him make his next move. He sank gradually into a troubled sleep, feeling alone in the world.

Chapter 22

It was still dark when Tom opened his eyes. In the light of a candle he dressed himself, and packed his rucksack with all his worldly goods. He put his apartment key in an envelope and, on his way out, slipped it into his landlord's letter box. Like the elephant's child who could smell the "Great Limpopo" from a distance, Jeremy and Jane Smith's child smelled the Thames, and he headed for it, due south.

The sun was rising on his left and the city was awakening when he found himself in Kensington Gardens. A powerful feeling of nostalgia gripped him as he recalled the stories of Peter Pan and Wendy and Tinker Bell and Captain Hook (who did a poep), which had thrilled his childhood in distant Africa. It seemed so familiar to him, just as J. M. Barrie had said it would be, just as Arthur Rackham had illustrated it. There was the River Serpentine, the Round Pond, and the Broad Walk; there were the rhododendrons, the rabbits, and, if Tom didn't look too carefully, the fairies formed from pieces of the first babies' laughter.

He rested on a park bench before continuing his journey south – past the Royal Albert Hall, past Imperial College, past Thurloe Station, past Onslow Square, and then, right, into Fulham Road. He was hungry and thirsty. He was anxious about how and where he would spend the night, and the next, and the next... He ogled the fresh fruit - Cape Apples - in the morning markets but his 'fieving' days were over.

Just before Fulham Road veered right, past Chelsea Football Club, Tom happened upon the entrance to Brompton Cemetery where many flower sellers were gathering. It then occurred to him that if he managed to avoid authority figures like sextons and security guards, he might just be able to secure free accommodation in the cemetery grounds. He remembered Dad's story about how he and his scouting friend, Dawid, had fled in terror from a graveyard, where was it? – somewhere near Howick in Natal. Smiling to himself, he sidled into the cemetery, which was vast, and began looking for a suitable camping site.

Brompton seemed more like a recreational park than a cemetery. By midday it was crowded with picknickers, bicyclists, tricyclists, scooterists, and pram pushers. There was no obtrusive officialdom, and Tom felt quite secure. He walked down a long colonnade flanked by catacombs to the domed chapel in the centre of the grounds. He was fascinated by the chapel door with its two winding serpents facing each other. He perused random tombstones, enjoying the familiarity of names like Mr Nutkins, Mr McGregor, Tod, Jeremiah Fisher, Tommy Brock, and Peter Rabbet.

His heart did a somersault when, late in the afternoon, he came upon the grave of Richard Tauber. He couldn't believe his eyes. It was beautifully kept, and someone had left a single yellow tulip on the granite slab around which cyclamens grew, some still flowering so late in the season. Tom took off his rucksack and squatted in order to read the inscription:

Richard Tauber
Born in Linz Austria 1891
Died in London 1948

"A golden singer with a sunny heart
The hearts delight of millions was his art
Now that rich, roaring, tender voice beguiles
Attentive angels in the land of smiles."
A.P. Herbert.

His heart swelled with images of his mother, not in a land of smiles, but a lonely house of half-knitted baby jumpers, half-read cowboy books, and half-remembered children; a house of sun-downers on the veranda listening to crude Rhodesian propaganda with a man who took her slavish loyalty for granted, a man magnanimous enough to forgive his family for his own transgressions; and Tom let fall a bitter tear.

There was a space at the head of Richard Tauber's grave which was large enough for him to lay out his sleeping bag, only it was too exposed to lurking officialdom; so Tom decided to make himself as inconspicuous as possible until darkness fell, when he would return to his chosen site. He put his rucksack back on and walked all the way up to the North, Old Brompton Road entrance. There he found a fairly secluded spot to rest, and soon fell asleep.

He was unceremoniously nudged awake by a security guard who told him that it would soon be closing time. Tom thanked him, and slowly retraced his steps in the direction of the Fulham Road entrance. The cemetery was being rapidly emptied of the living, which made Tom's presence increasingly conspicuous. He decided to try out the catacombs. Down there he was alone; and when he came across an empty recess, he leopard crawled in, backwards, pulling his knapsack along and using it to seal himself in, as it were.

He lay there, barely daring to breathe, for what seemed an eternity. Once, official sounding footsteps clomped down the passageway, but they did not hesitate at his tomb. After that, half an hour of complete silence decided Tom that the coast might be clear. He shuffled out of the recess, picked up his knapsack, and made his way to the surface. There was too much light around for him to walk upright so he leopard crawled from tombstone to tombstone. His years of camping in the Rhodesian bush had trained him to locate, almost instinctively, places he had pin-pointed, and he was soon back at the grave of the monocled Austrian gentleman, the great tenor, who had brought so much consolation over so many years to Jane Smith. Surreptitiously Tom laid out his sleeping bag, his cape too, because there were signs that it would rain later on. A barn owl called, and called intermittently while Tom sank slowly into the arms of Morpheus.

It was the scent which woke him first, a haunting blend of sandalwood and rose. Then the sounds, coming from a grave nearby; a large rat perhaps; or, surely not! - a corpse awakening! Before he could stop himself, Tom called out "Prema, shanti, ahinsa."

A woman's fearful voice replied, "Love, peace, kindness."

A soft rain had begun to fall. "Who's there?"

"Shit, it's going to rain." She had a mild cockney accent.

"I've got a cape."

"I'm scared. Are you a spook?"

"No, I'm real. I thought this hotel provided private accommodation."

"What can you expect when it's for free?"

"How come you knew my mantra?"

"I'm an Indian chick."

"Of course; your scent."

"It's chandan. I rinse my hair in it."

"Is your hair like a horse's tail?"

"Yes, it's long and strong and shiny and black."

"What's your name?"

"Shailja."

"That's pretty."

"What's yours?"

"Tom."

"That's schoolboyish. Oh dear, it's beginning to pour!"

"Quick. Come under the cape. It's big. I used it on my bike." She scrambled over and Tom covered them in the dependable yellow plastic. She was shivering. "Climb in." He held the sleeping bag open for her."

Without hesitation she squirmed in beside Tom. She was slender, almost skinny. She was dressed in some soft fabric, like a tracksuit. "It's a tight fit."

"You'll soon get warm. May I ask what you are doing spending the night in Brompton Cemetery?"

"You may. You smell like a girl."

"Elizabeth Arden products. I used to work at their factory in North Acton. I got fired yesterday."

"Does that explain why you are spending the night in Brompton Cemetery?"

"I guess so."

"Your accent. Are you from New Zealand?"

"No. Africa."

"Really? So am I. My family are from Uganda. I was born in Kampala."

"I was born in Gwanda."

"Where's that?"

"If I tell you will you promise not to abandon me?"

"It's not Rhodesia, is it?"

"I'm afraid so."

"You seem like a nice bloke, Tom, and I'm sure you didn't ask to be born there. After what happened to my people in Uganda, I'm not quick to judge other settlers. Why were you fired?" Tom told her his story starting from his first day at work when some accessories turned him into an accessory. "And you sent the stolen goods to your mother in Rhodesia?"

"Yes."

"That's sweet, Tom."

"What about you, Shailja? I'm sure you've got a more interesting story to tell."

"Not at all. I'm running away from an arranged marriage with an Indian bloke in Calcutta. My family have long tentacles in this city, so I have to hide in unusual places."

"What are your plans?"

"I have none. And you?"

"If I go home I'll be forced to re-join the army. Besides, I've sold my return ticket. If the British authorities get hold of me I'll be deported because I've been working illegally. So, no, I've got no plans beyond trying to survive another day."

She snuggled up to him. It was too dark for either of them to see each other's faces clearly. "Make a wish, Tom."

Tom thought for a bit and then said, "I wish I could show you my most favourite place in the world. It's called Nowhere. Do you wear Saris?"

"That's a bit of a non sequitur, but yes, I do, on family occasions."

"Are you a Hindu?"

"Yes, but I don't practise it. I like to think of myself as a free spirit. Actually, I'm a poet."

"Wow! That makes you special. Do you know 'When I am dead, my dearest...'"

"'Sing no sad songs for me...'". Christina Rossetti. One of my favourite poets."

"Wow!"

"Did you know that poem is engraved on her tombstone? She's buried in Highgate Cemetery."

"Highgate! But..."

"A group of us used to visit her grave on her birthday, and recite that poem." The rain had stopped, and the owl called again. Tom, bemused by coincidences, removed the cape, and they breathed in the sweetened air. "Well, Tom, your wish can't come true, not yet anyway; but there's no reason why mine can't."

"What is it?"

"To take you to a very special place in India."

"But Shailja, I'm completely broke!"

"That's no problem. My family owns half of London. I have my own bank account. Do you have a passport?"

"Yes. I managed to get a South African one through my parents. You can go virtually nowhere on a Rhodesian passport."

"That will do. Now let's get a good night's sleep because tomorrow is going to be a busy day making my wish come true."

"Where are you taking me?"

"To the most romantic place on earth."

"Where's that?"

"Be patient."

"May I touch your hair?"

"You may."

The touch soon became a gentle stroke. Her scent intoxicated him. "Who are you, Shailja?"

"I'm your woman, Tom; and you are my man. I read you in the stars."

EPILOGUE

Form and Content

My mother, Meg, was born in May,
her birthday cakes were shaped like a heart;
she smoked 100 cigarettes a day,
made us oxen out of clay,
preferred six eggs to a la carte.

Now that I'm past three score and ten
I watch the curtains ringing down,
and see the best laid schemes of mice and men
go wrong for want of acumen,
and find the bay leaves turning brown.

The low modality of May,
not hot, not cold, but almost warm;
my mother loved to read on such a day,
devouring J. T. Edson and Zane Grey,
savouring content, ignoring form.

My Earliest Memory

I'm sitting on a potty, smeared in blood,
playing with a blade I found on the floor;
my Mom's on the other side of the door
reading a cowboy book, chewing the cud,
sighing tobacco smoke. A white potty,
enamelled, scrapes against the cement;
tin handle buckled; here and there a dent.
I am three years old, my vest is snotty,

blotty. Crimson beads decorate my arm,
my leg, my feet, smudge the chamber pot.
She calls, are you ready, dear? I reply,
not knowing that I've done myself some harm
as the pretty jewels begin to clot.
She comes in - gives a primordial cry.

Threnody for My Mother

You determined who got the string
from the rolled roast beef,
the pope's nose, the crispier wing -
O the grief, the grief.

You decided on Christmas day
which crackers to pull,
whose turn it was, not Dad's, to pray -
O my heart is full.

You kissed us better in the night,
kissed for heaven's sake,
crossed the darkness with candle light
O the ache, the ache.

You healed our pets, you darned our socks,
nurtured every toy,
and now you whisper from the rocks -
O the joy, the joy.

Potato Bush

Boiled potatoes in their jackets is what
I think I smell. Mom is in the kitchen,
cowboy book with a cracked spine in one hand,
testing fork in the other; cigarette –
Springbok – between her lips. 'What's for supper,
Mom?' 'S and S,' she says, narrowing her
eyes to avoid the smoke. S and S – a
code we children could not crack, though we sensed
it meant 'whatever'.

But I am wandering down a river bed
dry as wrinkles, a month before the rains;
a bed of carapaces and driftwood,
a long season from my mother's kitchen;
and it's evening, and I know it now:
aartappelbos. It came to me once at
Punda Maria, once at Colleen Bawn,
once at West Nicholson. And I linger,
briefly overcome.

Our Last Night in Colleen Bawn

I thought that I had finished with this theme,
but I am haunted still by memories
of a time that never quite got started
and, clearly, will not have the grace to die.
I think of our last night in Colleen Bawn.
We sat on boxes in the dining room
polishing off the Old Man's brandewyn
and the seven hoarded tins of salmon
in tomato sauce. The conversation
ranged from life to death, the songs from 'Billy
Boy' to 'Blue Suede Shoes'. And then the dancing:
The Old Girl, solo, hitched her bra and shrugged
off thirty years. Round she goes. Round and round...
then up jumps Dad and takes her in his arms,
two-stepping the stuffing out of time: up
down, turn around, pump those elbows, bend those knees.
We stand to join the riot, when Gillie
bursts into tears and runs outside. We all
stop then; stop the talk, the singing, dancing,
drinking. And the crickets take over, and
a nightjar, and the distant tapping drums,
and, more distant still, the drone of traffic
on the Jo'burg Road. Then these take over.

Untwisting

The crop, crop, crop of my mother's scissors
(the pair we kids were not allowed to use)
cutting out dress patterns on the dining
room table, dropping ash, spitting the blues.

I can hear it all from my hiding place,
the laundry basket of my family smells;
curled like a clef on a stave, straining for
the ding dong daddiness of decibels.

Straining further, draped in sheets and under-
wear, for the chirp of the chalky grey tree
frog aestivating on the kitchen door,
untwisting discord into harmony.

Scrub Robin

1

I'm not reclining beneath a plum tree
on Hampstead Heath; I'm not about to fade
into oblivion. True, I can't see
what's going on about my feet displayed
in the season's first mud. They say the act
of observation changes whatever
is observed. Does that apply to birdsong?
Can sound be seen? Cool seepage soothes my cracked
heels as I, a Friday's child, endeavour
to locate it bob, bob, bobbin' along.

2

Then, it was Mopani scrub, that odour
of turpentine; the obliterating
chorus of cicadas; and always her
smoke-filled hours… lipstick, powdered cheeks… waiting
for the man with gorilla arms, and eyes
like cornflowers. Or singeing the firm-set
small feathers of a plump hen with the flames
from a twisted newspaper. Lullabies
to shoot the moon, to learn the alphabet;
counting – 1,2,3-4-5 - counting games.

3

In the morning, in the evening, rockin'
robin. Wrapping his flask of sweet, milky
tea with my Ouma's old Lisle stocking,
or part of the same newspaper, which she
used to singe the chicken, and which he reads
after work, on the stoep, from the back page
to the news, glass of Mainstay in his fist.
Ouma, vamping ain't we got fun, feeds
the cat on cream crackers, recalls her stage
debut in the roaring twenties, much missed.

4

Unlike the scrub robin that tweets the sun
when it rises and when it sets, she trips
to moonlit memories (one, two-three) of fun-
filled years after Delville Wood, while Mom strips
bed linen, and Dad files his fingernails,
and I, red mud squelching between my toes,
examine sickle bush thickets for eggs,
transforming whatever I observe: dales
into dongas, leas into bushveld, prose
into uncertain rhymes, lees into dregs.

5

Counting syllables while Dad remembers
Tobruk... rockin' robin... El Alamein...
white dust on his boots, hot desert embers
still glowing. Mom, tightly folding the pain
with her arms. Where will the cigarette ash
fall? Where will I find an untidy cup
of grass with protruding stems, neat lining,
and two freckled eggs? Suddenly a flash,
low-flying, skulking, you could say. Look up,
look down – gone. But listen to it pouring

6

forth its soul like moonlight when a fleeting
girl, colleen, lovely woman, took my hand
and placed it on a heart that stopped beating
for me when it stopped for her. Understand
that the act of observation alters
whatever is observed. I thought I saw
its tail, briefly, fanned, but it could have been
the detached wing of a moth, or the burrs
on a bush baby's rump, or a shrew's claw,
slightly curved, almost too small to be seen.

7

The mud has dried in scabs upon my feet;
I count the days, I count the minutes too;
I like to fantasize, to guess each sweet,
to wonder how I lost a girl like you;
but where's the use, this light-forsaken day,
of moaning like the wind that comes between
the song of dawn, the song of dusk… trilling
robin… of saying I loved you? Away!
Don't go! Away! I can't know what you mean:
observing eyes above cracked cheeks, spilling;

8

eyes seeping tears for what? For midnight?
I wonder if Ruth heard you in that field,
if she ever discerned the stripes, the white
tips, the rufous rump; and awake, I yield,
asleep, I yield, to whatever avails:
what I hear, what I see, and what I think
I know, is that the song of dusk, and dawn,
In this brown land is not the nightingale's
but the scrub robin's, and there is a link
holding what is cheerful and what forlorn.

ABOUT THE AUTHOR

Born in South Africa in 1947, John Eppel was raised in Zimbabwe, where he still lives, now semi-retired, in Bulawayo. With 20 books to his name, and contributions to numerous periodicals worldwide, John remains one of Zimbabwe's most prolific and creative writers with an individualist voice, tinged with biting satire. Several of John's poetry collections have won awards, including: *Spoils of War*, which won the Ingrid Jonker prize; *Landlocked: New and Selected Poems from Zimbabwe*, which was a winner in the international Poetry Workshop Prize judged by Billy Collins; and his NAMA award-winning collaboration with Togara Muzanenhamo, *Textures*. John won the MNet Prize in 1993 for his novel, *D G G Berry's the Great North Road*. His second novel, *Hatchings* was nominated for the MNet prize in 1993/4 and was chosen for the series in the *Times Literary Supplement* on the most significant books to have come out of Africa. In addition to his creative fiction, and building on his career as a teacher, John has also produced several study guides for O and A Level literature students.

ALSO BY JOHN EPPEL

FICTION
D.G.G. BERRY'S 'THE GREAT NORTH ROAD'
HATCHINGS
THE GIRAFFE MAN
THE CURSE OF THE RIPE TOMATO
THE HOLY INNOCENTS
ABSENT: THE ENGLISH TEACHER
TRAFFICKINGS
WHITE MAN WALKING

POETRY
FOUR VOICES *(WITH N.H. BRETTELL, ROLAND MOLONY, DAVID WRIGHT)*
SPOILS OF WAR
SONATA FOR MATABELELAND
SELECTED POEMS: 1965   1995
SONGS MY COUNTRY TAUGHT ME
HEWN FROM ROCK *(WITH PHILANI A. NYONI)*
TEXTURES *(WITH TOGARA MUZANENHAMO)*
LANDLOCKED: NEW AND SELECTED POEMS FROM ZIMBABWE
O SUBURBIA
TOGETHER *(WITH JULIUS CHINGONO)*

PROSE AND POETRY
THE CARUSO OF COLLEEN BAWN
WHITE MAN CRAWLING

Printed in the United States
by Baker & Taylor Publisher Services